"A smart, imaginative ride into the future where life hangs in the balance of diet and exercise."

Sarah McMurray, Owner/Director

Carriage House Children's School

"Nanoswarm puts science inside a captivating story, providing an effective way to teach both science and reading."

Leslie Miller, PhD

Senior Research Scholar

Center for Technology in Teaching and Learning

Rice University

"As a biologist and educator, I became engrossed in the story. I started thinking closely about my own eating habits and what I could be doing to better balance my energy levels during the day."

Lynnsey Dohmen

EcoStation & PowerPlay Educator

Children's Museum of Houston

2

NANOSWARM

Invasion From Inner Space

Mary Ann Pendino
Richard Buday, FAIA

Original story concept by Freeman Williams

This novella is based on *NANOSWARM: Invasion From Inner Space*, a video game adventure of healthy eating and exercise funded by the National Institutes of Diabetes and Digestive and Kidney Diseases of the National Institute of Health (grant number DK066724).

ISBN 978-0-578-03497-3
Edition 1.7, February 2010

www.Archimage.com/Nanoswarm.cfm

To my daughter Lucy and to a lifetime of healthy eating

for children everywhere.

Mary Ann Pendino

For Helen, who reminds me of Jessie.

Richard Buday

4100 Montrose Boulevard, Suite 200

Houston, Texas 77006

713.523.3425

www.Archimage.com

Contents

NANOTECH ROBOTS DELIVER GENE THERAPY THROUGH BLOOD

Sun, Mar 21, 2010 14:08 PM EDT

CHICAGO (Reuters) - U.S. researchers have developed tiny nanoparticle robots that can travel through a patient's blood and into tumors where they deliver a therapy that turns off an important cancer gene.

Prologue

In 2030, the global community took inventory. For the first time in the history of humankind, one could say the planet was at peace. Biomes around the world were flourishing. The cycles of life were operating with no interference. There were no wars. There was more than enough food. Most disease had been wiped out. The only remaining medical challenge was "Smart Germs."

Germs like *Staphylococcus percepi* could rapidly change their DNA structure when attacked by an antibiotic, rendering any drug useless. They did this through a process known as biomutation. The cycle was endless: a new disease would appear—an antibiotic would be developed—biomutation would change the germ, sometimes within days of encountering the antibiotic—and a newer, stronger form of the disease would emerge.

So far, Smart Germs were more of a nuisance than a serious public health threat. Scientists all over the world agreed, however, that one day, things would change. The only way to stop biomutation was to engineer antibiotics that were smarter than Smart Germs.

The Global Council turned to Earl Gunderson, MD, PhD, Director of the Miniaturization Exploration Center - Hardware Section, or what most people simply called MECHS. He and a dedicated staff designed the original nanobots, microbe-sized robots used for a variety of utilitarian functions. Nanobots recycled materials, cleaned up hazardous waste and generally helped around the planet with everyday chores. They even helped around the house. Carpet nanobots made sure rugs never had to be vacuumed. Clothing bots meant laundry machines were a thing of the past.

The Global Council identified Dr. Gunderson as the one scientist who could find a way to stop

biomutation and the rise of Smart Germs.
Gunderson's nanobot technology was the key.

MECHS Log - May 21, 2030

Today, I made significant progress in the
lab. My new version of nanobot model 200
successfully tracked down, identified and
destroyed viral bacteriophages in an E. coli
broth while leaving the E-coli bacteria
unharmed.

I feel the 207 may be the first step in
finding a defense against Smart Germs. Of
course, much more testing remains.

Earl Gunderson, MD, PhD, FACS, MBA
Director and Chief of Staff, MECHS

Orientation

There was never a time when I did not know about MECHS. My family had been a part of the center since its inception. My mother worked as a lab tech. My dad was a maintenance specialist. I always thought I would work there too, eventually. That day came sooner than expected.

I was still a teenager way back in 2030, a proud member of the "Nano Generation." I had been on the science track since I was ten. Unlike generations of the past, Nanogens were allowed to pick a career path as early as fifth grade. I chose science, or maybe it chose me. On my 13th birthday I completed F.A.Z.E. 1 of the science track. I graduated as a T1 at the top of my class with special honors in aviation. My dad liked to tell everyone that I passed with "flying" colors. He never could resist a good pun.

I knew I would go on to F.A.Z.E. 2 but I did not know where I would be stationed. I could be sent to Alaska to live in an ice-sealed biosphere or to a steamy rain forest on the equator. The thought of leaving friends and family was unsettling, but there was no way I could give up now. Besides, they wanted me to go. They wanted me to be successful, even if it meant leaving home.

My test scores and performance portfolio were sent to the Edutrust for review. Back then, Edutrust was a committee of great scientists appointed by universities from around the world. That was way before the Academe got democratized. Even so, the portfolio review process seemed more or less fair. F.A.Z.E. 2 candidates were reviewed by Edutrust and assigned the status of Trainee Second Class, or T2, at one of the global science institutes. Edutrust sent their final decisions to T1s via special messengers. It didn't matter if you passed or failed—you would receive a determination either way.

I was sitting on the front steps of our flat playing a computer game pad when the messenger arrived.

12

She was dressed in a black and gold uniform with a MECHS medallion embossed on her jacket. She handed me a small box. Inside was a PDA of some sort, but the coolest one I had ever seen.

Her instructions were to the point. "This is your personal Vitalink. Please key in your I.D. and follow the instructions on the screen." Then she asked me to place my thumb on the screen of her own Vitalink to acknowledge receipt of the delivery. She smiled as she turned to leave. "You and your family must be very proud."

As soon as I typed in my I.D. an image of a distinguished looking man popped up. "Well, congratulations on your recent promotion to Trainee Second Class. You will start F.A.Z.E. 2 on the aviation science track tomorrow. I'm Earl Gunderson, the Director of MECHS. Please report to the MECHS lab at 7 a.m. tomorrow morning for orientation."

I couldn't believe it! I had been assigned to MECHS. I wouldn't be leaving home after all. That evening my family and I celebrated at *Eaties*, an all-you-can-eat restaurant with food from all over the world. You could eat in Italy, Thailand and Mexico all in one night. It was the perfect place for a friends and family food party. And party we did.

I woke up the next morning with a food hangover. I figured it wouldn't affect my performance on my first day of training. I got up bright and early and caught the tram to the other side of town.

I'll never forget the way I felt when I walked up to the MECHS building for the first time. I stood at her base and looked straight up. She shot into the clouds with no end in sight. Standing in the shadows of this monolithic structure, I felt insignificant. It was very intimidating. MECHS was a towering fortress of concrete, glass and stainless steel. A huge MECHS medallion was etched deep in the middle of her solid belly. She stood for so much. I was humbled by her presence.

I must have seemed dazed because a couple of T3s came up behind me and tapped me on the shoulder.

"Hey, snap out of it!"

"Oh, sorry. I was just..."

Yeah, yeah, we know," said the girl. "We did the same thing when we first got here."

"No big deal," the boy added. "It's just a building. And that thing over there? That's just the door."

I recognized the girl right away. It was Jessie Crowfoot. I'd seen her picture on news vids. Jessie had become something of a celebrity this past year. Jessie was one those "wunderkinds," the highflying genius types that MECHS seems to attract. Not a bad term to describe a pilot. Jessie was only a year ahead of me in the science track, but I had heard she was working on a special project, something really hush-hush. I didn't recognize the boy. They passed me and walked inside.

"Hey," Jessie yelled back, "orientation will be straight down that corridor on your left. You can't miss it. See you later aviator."

Aviator? How did she know that? I pulled myself together and walked inside. The place was filled with people—talking in groups, walking here and running there. Man, this was a busy place! Still, the overall environment seemed calm and ordered. The walls were covered with a wash of gentle white light. The floor was made of something that I had never seen before. It felt like cushions below my feet, yet I did not sink into the floor as you might expect. It seemed like the place was designed to keep people happy and productive.

I stopped for a moment and gazed at the people around me. I wondered if I would be up to the challenge. Not everyone makes it here. Happy or not, MECHS had the reputation of being one of the hardest centers in any science track. Rumor had it that only one or two percent of all T2s make it to T3 here. Will I be one of them? Too early to tell, I figured.

An announcement brought me back to reality. "All T2s, please report to the orientation center. T2s to the orientation center."

I collected my thoughts and walked down the hall in the direction Jessie suggested. On the way, I placed my doubts on a "mental shelf." The mental shelf was a technique I learned in T1 training. We all have doubts and fears. The key is not to avoid them while, at the same time, not giving into them. By putting them on a shelf we acknowledge their presence. When they start to bother us, all we have to do is put them back on the shelf. That day, my fears were on the shelf.

I entered the orientation center with about twenty other new T2s. They separated us into small groups and assigned us interview pods. I found mine and, as I approached, a small metal arm extended from the wall. The door behind me closed and a computerized female voice told me to place my Vitalink into a receptacle on the arm. Then, a projected vid with a human outline appeared on the wall.

"Welcome to the Vitascan, Trainee," a computerized female voice instructed. "Please step forward and stand with your back to the scanner. Please remain still while the Vitascan links to your Vitalink and reads your biometric signature." The Vitascan's sensor beam swept my body from head to toe.

"Please stop looking around," she said. "And try to relax." This computer was pretty observant.

I guess us newcomers all had the same look on our faces, like seeing the ocean or a mountain for the first time. Well, it was hard to believe that someplace as incredible as this existed.

"We will now perform an initial energy scan. Breathe in... breathe out... now hold your breath... Thank you. Please breathe normally." A minute later she said, "You may now remove your Vitalink."

The arm retracted and was replaced by a small keyboard and input pad. A large holographic vid descended from above.

"Please fill out this intake questionnaire. The information will serve as a baseline profile for your training. Please be honest and exact. You may begin."

The questionnaire focused on personal values, how much I ate, what I ate, when I exercised. What any of this had to do with aviation or science was a mystery to me, but it wasn't the time to question the MECHS approach. I answered the questions and waited for my next instruction.

"Thank you. Interim questionnaires will be requested as your training progresses. Now, please direct your attention to the screen in front of you. There is an incoming message from your team leader, Jessie Crowfoot."

I thought I was hearing things. Jessie Crowfoot was my team leader? No way I would be working with someone like her!

A holograph of the young girl I saw outside the MECHS building appeared. "Hi, aviator. I'm Jessie and you're on my team. Welcome aboard. I'm expecting great things from you."

18

Next, a clean-cut African American guy appeared. "Hey Trainee, wipe that daze off your face. I'm Demetrius Johnson. I like your energy. You seem confident but your doubts get in the way at times. I can help you with that."

Say what? How did he know about my struggle with self-doubt? What else did he know about me?

Another person appeared. "Hello, I'm Roberto Rodriguez. I've been reviewing the results of your intake questionnaire. You and I have a lot of work to do."

Okay, I thought to myself, exactly what does that mean? One more team member appeared, the boy who was with Jessie. "So you're the one who's gonna replace me, huh? Just kidding. I'm Fred Walters and I'm delighted to have another pilot on the team. These nanobrains expect me to fly them everywhere."

"Don't listen to Fred. He's a joker." Yet another person on the vid. "I'm Elena Sanchez. I like to think of myself as the only sane one around here. Berto never laughs, Fred laughs too much, and Dee... well, you'll see."

Jessie reappeared on the screen. "This is your team. Sorry, but you're stuck with us for a while.

We're taking you out to lunch today. Meet us outside the MECHS front door when you're done with orientation. See you later, Wings."

An hour of computer-based questions later, the female voice told me, "This concludes your orientation. Please be sure that you begin reading the MECHS manual that was downloaded to your Vitalink. You are asked to read the first sixty pages by tomorrow. The Trainee is dismissed."

Sixty pages? I would be up all night reading that. Oh well, no one said being a T2 would be easy. Still in a daze, I met the others outside.

"How many pages do you have to read?" Fred asked, first looking at Jessie then at me.

"Sixty."

"Ouch! That's ten more than it use to be." Turning back to Jessie, Fred said, "I don't know why they think new trainees have more brain capacity than we did at the start of training."

"Fred," Jessie said with a wide grin, "I don't think we should use your brain capacity as any kind a measure. Come on Wings, let's take a quick tour of the lab before we go to lunch."

"Um... Wings?" I asked.

"Yeah, Jessie likes to give everyone a nickname," Elena explained. "Robert is Berto. Demetrius is Dee. Get used to it."

"Hey, I got a nickname for you Jessie," Fred said. "From now on, ye shall be known as Tomahawk!"

Apparently, Fred enjoyed teasing Jessie about her Native American heritage. Her great grandfather was a tribe elder, something of a legend within the Indian Nation. Jessie was lightly built but very strong, and just as strong willed. Fred was less interesting, your basic slightly overweight kid from the suburbs. These two could not have been more different, yet something about their eyes gave them a funny resemblance. They say you can tell a lot about a person by looking at their eyes. Fred's eyes were round. Jessie's were shaped like almonds. But when they smiled, their eyes were identical. Maybe that's why they were able to insult each other so often and still remain friends. Obviously, they had known each other a long time.

We went back inside MECHS and turned right this time, toward the labs. At the end of the hall was a security door. Jessie placed her hand on a biosensor to the right of the door and it slid open instantly. We walked into a round space with corridors running in every direction. Straight ahead was a glass bridge.

"This way," Jessie pointed.

Looking down, I could see we were easily fifty feet above a huge factory of sorts. Workers dressed in sanisuits peered into what looked like tiny Petri dishes. Technicians labored at stations building... something... I couldn't be sure what. Was that a micro scanner? The drawing on that vid seems to be a nano power unit schematic.

Then it dawned on me. I was standing on top of the famous "Bot Shop." Unbelievable! This was the place where nanobots of all shapes, sizes and special applications were designed, built and shipped all over the world. Most people never even got a chance to see pictures of the Bot Shop much less take a tour. Nanobot production was a closely guarded secret back then, not at all like today. Only Dr. Gunderson had access to the complete engineering model. Why shouldn't he? He was the one who developed it. Nanobots were his babies and the Bot Shop is where they were born.

At the end of the bridge was a thick stainless steel door inscribed with a not so friendly sign

AUTHORIZED PERSONNEL ONLY. Jessie put her hand again on a biosensor. Again, the door opened and we entered. I looked around the place in amazement.

"Welcome home." Jessie said to me. "Go ahead. Check it out."

I walked around, sliding my hand over the workstation consoles. I was familiar with some of the equipment, but most of it was a mystery to me. A small pad, it actually looked like a landing pad but was too small and had way too much extra equipment around it, sat in the middle of the room. And there was lots of other exotic looking equipment. A nameplate on one workstation caught my eye: EARL GUNDERSON, MD, PHD, FACS, MBA.

"This is Dr. Gunderson's lab?" No way a T2 like me should be here. Jessie and her friends were probably pulling a practical joke. Maybe it was a cruel initiation trick. I was heading for the door when Fred stopped me.

"Hold up, Wings. Where do you think you're going? You are part of Gunderson's research lab now. We all are."

It couldn't be true, could it? Dr. Gunderson only chose one T2 a year to work in his lab. One! I found it hard to believe he would choose me. I'm a pretty good pilot, but that's hardly the same as a research scientist prodigy. Then again, MECHS wasn't known for making mistakes. Where did I put that mental shelf?

Suddenly there was a scream from the other side of the lab. Out of the corner of my eye, I saw Jessie duck behind a wall. Fred was in close pursuit, chasing her with some kind of mechanical thing. Turned out it was just a large-scale prototype for a new nanobot, but it looked like a huge, 1-foot wide insect. Jessie counterattacked by grabbing a flask off Gunderson's workstation. She uncorked it and waved it under Fred's nose.

Fred recoiled at the smell. "Yuk! Gross! What is that?"

Jessie grinned and turned the flask around. The label read: MEDIBOT EXPERIMENT #207.

"Medibot?" Elena asked. "What is that? Some kind of Mediterranean vacation for robots?"

Everyone laughed and the tension quickly disappeared. Still, I couldn't figure out why Jessie had gotten so upset. It was just a nanobot model and besides, she was a superstar. I didn't think anything could "bug" her.

I found out later that Jessie had been bitten by a brown recluse spider when she was four years old. She had almost died. Since then, she's been deathly afraid of bugs. Who wouldn't be after an experience like that? The sight of anything spider-like instantly switched her into panic mode. It was just about the only thing in the world that could scare her. Jessie was working hard on overcoming her arachnophobia (the scientific name for her fear of spiders), but Fred wasn't helping things. In fact, he seemed to enjoy tormenting her about it.

Those two had a strange relationship, no doubt about it. Sometimes they were the best of buddies. Sometimes they were fierce competitors. They spent a lot of time teasing and taunting each other. The whole thing was weird.

The team decided to go to *Eaties* for lunch. Fred wanted to take the tram, but Berto said it would be better for us to walk.

"With our feet?" Fred protested. "What's wrong with you guys? Nobody walks anymore. It's so pedestrian." But Fred reluctantly agreed.

On the way to *Eaties*, Berto showed me some games on his Vitalink. They were a little different from the games you could play on a game pad. These were MECHS games, and Berto had designed most of them himself. I'd never met anyone who actually developed a computer game before. Berto gave me my first tutorial. He called the game, "LEDGE."

"Basically," he said, "LEDGE is a zero-sum game. It's all about maintaining the balance between the foods you eat and the energy you expend. Look."

Berto took the Vitalink from my belt and punched up the main menu. A few clicks later, an empty plate appeared in the middle of the screen.

"So, here's this plate. The object is to construct one of your typical meals by choosing foods from the side of the screen and dragging it to the plate. You have control over portion size. All you do is slide the handle next to the plate. See?"

Berto was obviously proud of his creation. "Click the Next button when you're ready to add more food," he said. "Your selection moves to the bottom of

26

the screen. When you're done adding food, click the FINISHED button."

I hit the button.

"The vertical bar on your right is the energy balance meter. If it stays in the middle, your energy is balanced and you can go on to the next part of the game. If it doesn't balance, you have to make some adjustments either to your intake or output. You do that by changing your food selection or portion size. You can also add food or delete food. If you want, you can exercise to burn energy by selecting your favorite exercises. There's even a clock to adjust the amount of time you engage in your chosen activity."

I told Berto that LEDGE didn't seem like too much of a challenge. "So, where's the fun in this?" I asked.

He grinned and said, "It's not as easy as it looks. Anyway, this is just the setup level. The challenge begins after you get through energy balance. From here, you enter the dark world of LEDGE. Each time you play, the world changes. How well you balanced your energy determines whether you live or die in the game." Berto's tone turned a little scary. "Wanna play a little game?" Berto was right. LEDGE looked easy, but it was harder than I thought. Balancing energy in and energy out is complicated. We played LEDGE all the way to *Eaties*, although I didn't even make it to the first level. I was stuck in setup. Berto, on the other hand, danced through three entire LEDGE worlds. "Think I'll add some more levels after lunch," he said.

The more time I spent with Berto, the more impressed I became with his intellect. Berto was a born research scientist. He could look at cold hard facts and uncover the ground truth that connected them. He was also a mathematical wizard, which may have been why he sometimes had a hard time dealing with Dee. Dee was Berto's complete opposite. Berto viewed life as an equation. Anything you could see could be analyzed and scientifically modeled. If you couldn't see it, it didn't exist.

In contrast, Dee operated on intuition. Mathematics didn't matter. Things you could see were boring. Dee thought more about things you could never detect with instruments. Feelings for instance, invisible waves of energy that could only be understood with your eyes closed. There was a rumor that Dee was clairvoyant. That means the power to see without eyes, to smell without a nose, to know what's going to happen before it does. I didn't believe it either, but Dee's world did seem beyond the range of most people's normal senses. He always knew what the rest of us were thinking, and sometimes that got a little creepy. I got the feeling that Berto didn't trust Dee very much.

I must have built up an appetite because when we got to *Eaties* I raced through the international smorgasbord like a turbocharged racehorse. I filled my plate with fish and chips from Britain, tacos from Mexico, pasta from Italy, and potatoes from Germany. You name it; I put it on my plate. When we sat down to eat I looked at the others' plates. Fred's was the only one that matched mine. Everyone else had much smaller portions.

Jessie stared at the pile of food on my plate, then at the pile of food on Fred's plate. She looked me straight in the eyes and said, "You and Fred must be cousins."

"I think we need to start over, Wings." Berto jumped up from his chair. "Come on, I'll help you." Berto took my full tray of food to an empty table and left it there. He guided me back through the food line and started talking. To achieve energy balance in the real world, I would have to spend some time thinking about food choices, portion sizes, and substituting unhealthy menu items for healthier ones. I would also have to look at my water intake and add physical activity to my daily routine. These ideas were not completely foreign to me. All T1s had to take a health and fitness course as part of the general curriculum. I understood the concept but I didn't apply it as well as I should have. I don't know why. Lack of time or the bother of it all, I guess. It was faster and easier to grab a combo meal on the run somewhere than it was to pick out healthy things to eat, or so I thought. And my exercise routine was, well, not exactly a routine. More like catch-as-catch-can.

"All of us really have to stay in shape to meet the challenges and demands of the MECHS program," Berto said. It sounded like an advertisement, but Berto fully meant it. Berto rarely kidded around.

Luckily, I would not be expected to change all of my habits at once. I could set one goal at a time and work with it until it became a part of my daily routine. I would always have the support of the team, Roberto assured me. He suggested we set my first goal together. Scientist that he was, he said that we start with baseline data.

"You probably learned a lot of this in T1 training, Wings. I hope it's not too boring. Let's begin."

I did remember some of it. A standard portion was about the size of my fist, except for leafy vegetables. That was two fist sizes. Macaroni and cheese was not a vegetable. Too much sweetened juice was not good for you.

"So," Berto asked, "what do you want to add to your diet this week as a goal? Fruit or vegetable?"

I wanted to add ice cream but guessed Berto wouldn't find that funny. I chose an apple. I figured apples were pretty easy to find and you could eat them on the run if you had to.

There was something empowering about the process. I felt good about it. I realized that I would be learning a lot of new and wonderful things at MECHS. I just hoped that I would be up to everything else they threw at me.

Berto congratulated me on setting my first goal. We went back to our table with my healthy tray and joined the others. As I sat down I noticed Fred didn't look well. Dee thought he might be coming down with something. That suspicion was confirmed when Fred said he was feeling light headed.

"I don't see how any one could feel good after eating all that," Jessie said, pointing to Fred's plate. She clearly enjoyed rubbing it in.

Fred let out a long grunt. "Get over it, Tomahawk. I just need to... uh..."

Fred's face turned white. He got out of his chair, took a few steps, and then hit the floor face down.

Jessie jumped out from her chair. "What the...? Fred, what are you doing?"

The rest of us ran to Fred and fell to our knees, forming a circle around him. Dee flipped Fred on his back and Elena lifted his head. Beads of sweat were on his forehead. His eyes were closed but he wasn't asleep. He was shivering. We stared at each other in disbelief. Thirty seconds later, Fred stopped shaking and went limp. He was out cold.

Crisis

I mumbled something to Berto about the Heimlich maneuver. He looked at me and said, "No, Fred isn't choking on food." Berto gently lowered Fred's head back down to the floor. He put his hands on his chest and was just about to start CPR when he noticed, "He's still breathing." He put his head to Fred's chest. "It's slow, but he's breathing."

Dee slid over and tried to analyze Fred's bio-functions with his Vitalink. "Stupid biometrics!" He got only a blank screen. "Berto... why won't this work?"

"You can't link to him without his permission. Security, remember? But Jessie can. She's on his buddy list."

"There's no buddy list on Vitalinks," Dee said.

"There is now. I made some changes."

Jessie grabbed her Vitalink and scanned Fred. Dee pointed his Vitalink at the food Fred was eating. Me, I stayed out of the way. I was amazed at the choreography of the moment. Everyone seemed to know just what to do.

"Pulse is high," Jessie reported. "Clammy to the touch... blood sugar high... O2 low."

"Nothing wrong with the food," Dee said.

Elena lifted Fred's head from the floor. "We gotta try and stabilize him."

Berto stood up. "He's out like a light. I.. I don't know what else to do. We should get him to Dr. Gunderson stat!"

Elena radioed for an emergency transport.

Everything had changed so quickly. We were all having fun, eating, talking, and then this. Fred was chowing down one moment, passing out the next. The whole thing was surreal.

The transport arrived and whisked Fred away. Berto and Jessie went with him. The rest of us caught the city tram. Even though there were plenty of empty seats, we stood up. Nobody said a word. I don't know about you, but to me, silence can be nerve racking. Yet, what can you say at a time like this? Instead, I looked at everyone's eyes. What I saw was worry. I started to get worried myself.

I had to break the silence. "Shouldn't Fred be going to a hospital instead of back to MECHS?" After all, the doctors there..."

"Are not as good as Dr. Gunderson." Dee emphatically cut me off. "How are you coming with your goals, Wings?"

"What?" I was surprised to hear about goals at a time like this, and I told Dee so.

"No Wings, you got it wrong." Anytime is a good time to think about goals. Now is a great time, especially since it will give us all a chance to think and calm down."

Dee must be reading my mind. He knows I'm afraid.

"I know Berto helped you set a goal for the week," Dee said. "Did he tell you we also use our Vitalinks to keep up with goals? Let me show you how to update the Vitalink with your goal status."

When we got to MECHS, we found Jessie and Berto propping up Fred on the lab's Vitascan. Dr.

Gunderson had a blood probe on Fred's arm and was running tests. Jessie reviewed the data as soon as it came out of the Vitascan and reported it to Gunderson. Fred was still unconscious. The rest of us stayed out of the way and waited for instructions.

A few minutes later, Dr. Gunderson walked over to me and introduced himself. "Guess there's no better way to learn to swim than being tossed into a pool," he said. He stuck out his hand. "Happy to have you on board. I am looking forward to working with you... once things settle down around here."

Gunderson walked back to the Vitascan. A series of 3-dimensional scans were being generated on computer monitors. It was like a slide show of Fred's insides. The show started at his head and began to slowly move down, centimeter by centimeter. It was awesome. Perfect images of his brain and spinal chord appeared. His heart was a magnificent machine. It was expanding to take in rushing blood from his veins and contracting to push out purified blood through his arteries. Truly, I thought, the heart is a miracle of engineering. Hopefully, the scans would soon reveal what happened to Fred.

Readings from the biosensor in his Vitalink showed that everything came at once. Some health conditions are like that. You don't know you have the problem inside you until it's too late. But hours passed with no informative data. Everyone was frustrated. Then Jessie noticed something on the Vitascan monitor. Something was moving, something that was not part of a human structure. She zoomed in. There were tiny moving objects, hundreds of them, in Fred's blood stream. They were swarming and linking together like a train, moving about Fred's abdomen in a spiral motion.

Jessie stared at the screen. "Dr. Gunderson, is this..."

Gunderson and Berto turned around in their chairs. We all stared at the monitor. You could have heard a pin drop. The team was in shock. I had no idea what we were looking at, but they did.

Gunderson spoke first. "I don't believe what I'm seeing."

Jessie hesitated for a moment before she said, "Tell me these aren't what I think they are.

Gunderson was still thinking. Seemed like he was trying to draw some kind of conclusion but you could see confusion in his face.

Jessie asked again. "Please?"

Gunderson took a deep breath and said, "They're bots."

Nanobots? You could almost hear the wheels grinding in our minds. Bots. I had to repeat the word several times in my head. What were nanobots doing inside Fred? Shivers went down my spine as I watched hundreds of nanobots swarm through Fred's bloodstream. I thought I felt something jab me in the stomach. It was probably just sympathy pains, but I couldn't help wonder what was going on inside my own body.

Gunderson started directing the team like the conductor of an orchestra. He told Berto and Dee to put Fred in a flight suit and lower him in the hydrotank, a large glass vessel in the corner of the lab. Jessie made a saline solution for the tank with the same properties as seawater. Elena connected hoses and cables from the Vitascan to the tank. I helped out wherever I could.

Fred's flight suit was very interesting. It wasn't like any suit I had trained in—more like a wet suit with a helmet than anything else. I wondered if it was part of a MECHS project. As fate would have it, I was about to find out.

Fred was soon floating peacefully in the hydrotank. Gunderson said the saline solution would create a stable environment for him. The tank's stasis system would slow down the normal flow of blood through Fred's body and keep the bots from spreading too quickly. The tubes and cables would be used to copy energy to Fred. All of this would keep him alive while the rest of us figured how to get the bots out.

Of course, I'm still thinking, how did bots get inside Fred? Everyone knows it's against basic bot programming to enter a human body. It's a fundamental rule of nanobot behavior. Nanobots are hard coded to do no harm. Heck, I thought nanobots couldn't even survive in the bloodstream. They would break down, dissolve or be eaten by our own antibodies. I also didn't understand Gunderson's strategy. Copy energy? What did that mean? I knew from my studies that energy has to have a source. The sun is a source of heat energy. Water is a source of potential energy, although you have to convert it to get kinetic energy. But, what kind of energy was Gunderson going to copy to Fred?

Then the answer came. Gunderson asked me to stand on the Vitascan. The energy source wasn't a "what" at all, it was a "who." It fact, it was me! Actually, all of us—Jessie, Berto, Elena, Dee—all of us would be Fred's energy source. Gunderson explained that energy transfer was sort of like a blood transfusion without blood. The Vitascan would replicate our energy profile and download it into Fred. It was like copying part of a computer file and pasting it into another document. The original file remained intact but the new document shared its contents.

The Vitascan read my energy. Data was displayed as bars on its screen. Each bar represented different aspects of my energy profile. A percentage rating system from 0 to 100 was on the left hand side of the graph. In some ways, the screen looked like Berto's LEDGE game. It was real life imitating computer art. Like LEDGE, there are consequences in the real world if you don't maintain energy balance. But in LEDGE, only the game avatar dies, not the actual player. I had the sinking feeling that Fred could die.

Fred's suit was also equipped with biosensors. His readout was displayed next to mine. Gunderson said his levels were stable. There was no need to copy my energy just yet, but my levels were stored on the storage drive for reference.

The videophone rang in Gunderson's office. The rest of us looked through the glass wall that separated his workstation from the lab. The face on the monitor looked very familiar. Could that be...? Of course! It was the President of the United States, Margaret Crane. She was talking to Dr. Gunderson. This wasn't just a prerecorded clip on an evening news vid. They were actually talking to each other. They knew each other! I must have looked astonished because Dee put his hand on my shoulder and said, "Hey, it's okay. She calls him all the time." I guess the rest of them were used to it by now.

Gunderson looked upset when he came out of his office. I wondered if it was because of Fred or if he always felt that way after speaking to the president. He told us that he had to leave for an emergency meeting at the White House. He told us to keep the news vid on because the president was going to address the nation in a couple of hours. We were to stay close to the lab until further notice.

Man, this was something. In just half a day, I had been assigned to a team headed by a world-renowned scientist, watched a new friend pass out in an all-you-can-eat restaurant and seen the President of the United States videoconference with my new boss. That's a lot for a new trainee, but I had a funny feeling I was sailing past the tip of a really, really big iceberg.

Berto suggested we take time out to chill in the LifePad, maybe even get a snack. Elena had to pry Jessie from her guard position at the hydrotank. Jessie was glued to the glass wall separating her from Fred. She didn't want to leave him. She kept mumbling something under her breath. I couldn't quite hear what she was saying, but at one point it sounded like "my fault." I didn't know what she was talking about and I didn't feel like I knew her well enough to ask.

Dee stayed at the main console. "I'm gonna meditate for a while. Someone make me a smoothie, will ya."

The MECHS lab was rather large. The LifePad was an adjacent room where team members could relax. It was fully equipped with a state-of-the-art computerized snack bar. You could get soups, salads, sandwiches, pizza by the slice, practically anything. There was also a smoothie bar.

Berto made everyone a fruit smoothie. We sat there drinking, no one saying anything. There was that silence again. It was like when you have a family member in the hospital and everyone is waiting for the doctor to come in and tell you what's going on. Everyone is too scared to speak.

There were also a couple of computers in the LifePad. Berto explained that you could use them to calculate your energy balance, or "EB" as he called it, before you ate. All you had to do was select foods like you did in LEDGE and the computer would do the rest. Berto guided me through the process.

"Watch, I'll show you how this works," he said. "Try ordering a cheeseburger and fries. Now activate your Vitalink. It will log your biosensor into the snack bar server. The screen shows your energy balance and the impact the cheeseburger would have on it. You can reassemble your meal until your energy is balanced. Go ahead. Give it a go."

I did exactly as he said, and was shocked by the results. Apparently the meal I almost had at *Eaties* would have taken its toll. I took the cheese off a burger. It wasn't enough. I took off the bun. Not enough. I substituted fries with a fruit cup. I was almost there. The data showed if I walked for thirty minutes I could balance for the day. What about dinner? I'd be out of balance again. Berto told me not to sweat dinner. I had a version of the EB program on my Vitalink. I could check it out when I got home. I played with a couple more menu items and finally settled on a grilled chicken salad with super spicy dressing. I love spicy food. I love lots of flavor. Heck, I just love food.

The salad thing was not something I would usually choose. I continued having doubts about making it through T2 training. Berto must have noticed the look on my face because he gave me some unsolicited encouragement.

"Listen Wings, don't worry about it too much. It's not hard, but it is important. The work we do at MECHS can wear a person down. Your body needs to be able to handle the stress that comes with being on the team. Look at Fred. Nobody's saying it, but I can't help think that he brought this on himself."

Jessie turned and snapped. "Don't knock Fred, Berto."

"I'm not knocking him, Jessie. I just think that maybe he..."

"So stop thinking so much." Jessie stormed off toward the lab.

"She knows I'm right," Berto said softly. "The only reason Gunderson keeps giving Fred extra time to get the eating-exercise thing right is because he is a great pilot. And we need a great pilot here, but the team can't wait forever. That may be why you were brought up so fast, Wings."

Ah ha, I thought.

"And it's a good thing you were because Fred can't fly anything in the hydrotank, now can he?" Berto looked at Jessie looking at Fred in the hydrotank. "Anyway, Fred's condition isn't your concern. Just follow the program. As Dr. Gunderson is fond of telling us, set your goals and meet them. That's all you have to do. Come on let's find something healthy to snack on."

The newness of being at MECHS was wearing off. Reality was setting in. I hadn't made it through the first day and I was already feeling the pressure. I remembered what it was like during T1 training. It was hard work. Yeah, I know, everything is hard work, but life as a T2 was turning out to be something else again.

Jessie stayed at the hydrotank staring at Fred. Elena checked the tank and made a few adjustments. Dee kept meditating. Berto sat on the Vitascan playing LEDGE. I walked around the lab wondering what everything did but tried not to touch anything important looking.

"Ah, go ahead. It's your lab too." He did it again! How does Dee know what I'm thinking? Geeze, he was good at that.

The lab had some familiar objects: the usual work station consoles, Petri dishes, flasks and the like. Even the hydrotank wasn't too unusual. I had seen one before during T1. I opened a few drawers and cabinets. Nothing out of the ordinary. Then I looked again at that strange platform in the middle of the lab. It really did look like a landing pad but it was smaller than most aircraft pads I had seen. And what's with all

46

that equipment around the perimeter? I saw what looked like a hangar door behind the pad, but even that was too small to wheel an aircraft through. I wondered if there was some other sliding panel in the roof or something. But we were on the first floor and there was a monster building on top of us. Must be something else, I thought to myself. The MECHS lab was big, but not big enough to have aircraft flying around. So, what's a hangar door doing in a lab, then? I thought about asking Dee about the pad and what was behind the hangar door when my lab tour was suddenly interrupted.

An emergency news vid signal went off behind us. We turned around and stared at a vid on the wall above a row of consoles. The vid had automatically switched itself to the National Emergency Broadcasting channel when the signal went up. On the screen was a picture of the White House. The vid's feed bar said this was going out to every news vid in the country. Then the president appeared. Standing next to the president was Dr. Gunderson.

"My fellow Americans, I am addressing the nation today to make you aware of a recently discovered and potentially dangerous situation.

As you know, our world has come to depend on nanotechnology for everything from cleaning polluted water to washing laundry. But, now there is a problem. Nanobots are attacking people."

Dee looked at me. Berto looked at Elena. Jessie turned back to Fred in the hydrotank.

"Hospitals all over the country are admitting patients suffering from a variety of symptoms including shortness of breath, dizziness, sweating, thirst, and in some cases seizures. Tests show swarms of nanobots in their bloodstream. If you or any one you know begins to exhibit these symptoms please go to the nearest hospital emergency room immediately." She went on about how nobody has died yet, but you could tell by the look on her face that she was worried about that. Then she introduced Dr. Gunderson, the inventor of nanobot technology.

"I want to assure you" he said, "that we are doing everything in our power to address this problem. I promise, we will not fail you."

Fade to black. Then a bunch of news people talking about what they had just heard replaced the image of Dr. Gunderson and the president. Dee turned the vid off.

So, it wasn't just Fred. It was happening to people all over the country. We were in a national emergency and MECHS was smack in the middle. Wait a second. I was in the middle of a national emergency! I just got here. I was barely a T2. I hadn't learned anything yet, but I was squarely in the middle of this thing!

Jessie turned her attention from Fred and looked at Dee. Dee looked as if he already knew what Jessie was thinking. I started thinking that now would be an excellent time to panic.

Gunderson called a meeting when he returned from the White House and laid out a plan of action. First, he ran Vitascans of us all to make sure Fred was the only MECHS team member with a bot infection. We were clean. Then he assigned Dee to continue collecting data from Fred. Berto and Elena were to download patient data from hospitals around the country and try to find common denominators. I would be replacing Fred as pilot.

Huh? The pilot of what? I had been accepted into MECHS' aviation sciences, but I had seen zero aircraft around here so far.

Gunderson told me that I would be working with Jessie, a first class pilot in her own right. I had always heard stories about Jessie Crowfoot and the Flyer, a two-person craft that handled like a sports car at high speeds and hovered like a hummingbird. It could fly through the air and, with a flip of a switch, dive nose first into water. It was the most versatile ship in the world. Jessie designed the Flyer and MECHS built it. Maybe her Flyer is...

"Okay Wings, we got work to do." Jessie took me to the hangar door behind the landing pad and pressed a button. The panel rolled up.

Behind the panel was small room with half of a cockpit of—I was right—the Flyer. This was a Flyer simulator. We got into the seats. Some of the controls and gauges were the same as in any flying machine but most were like nothing I had ever seen before.

Jessie booted the simulator. After 30 seconds of flashing lights, a logon message appeared on a screen in the center console. "Welcome to the Flyer simulator. Please enter your MECHS I.D. and password." I was about to start Flyer training. I'm talking about the Flyer. Jessie's Flyer.

"How about we use WINGS for your password. You can change it later if you want. Enter your MECHS I.D. and get ready for the ride of your life."

Jessie took the controls. She flipped a switch and the panel rolled down. A dome-shaped virtual screen descended from above. It was amazing. Everything was so lifelike. I felt like I could touch the clouds when we were up in the sky and swim with fish when we were in the ocean. She was right. It was the ride of my life, and it was over too fast.

"Next time, you fly. See you tomorrow. Don't forget about your goal setting. Later, Wings."

At last, my first day at MECHS was over. I don't know how I made it through, but I did. I looked at Fred on the way out. He looked peaceful in there. I wondered if he had any idea what was going on inside him, or even around him and the country. We had all been through a lot today, but no one here had gone through as much as Fred, even if he didn't know it.

When I got home, my family had a million questions. Mom made a special dinner to celebrate my first day at MECHS. I loved her fried chicken and mashed potatoes. I usually would have wolfed them down, but I knew I shouldn't eat as much as I usually do. Not after today. Not if I want to maintain EB. I realized that if I was gonna balance my energy for the day I had better substitute the mashed potatoes with a salad. I felt pretty good about the decision. It wasn't perfect, but at least I was moving in the right direction.

I remembered the goal I had set: one apple a day. We didn't have any apples so I ate a pear instead. I figured substituting my goal fruit with another was better than not eating fruit at all. I asked Mom to buy some apples for the week. She said she would.

After dinner I ran a bioscan using my Vitalink on each member of my family. I checked everyone's EB. My little brother Joey was borderline. I talked with him and my parents about making some changes. We all agreed our family menus could use some improvement. We also agreed to set a family goal for the week: buy and eat apples for dessert instead of ice cream. I was not popular, but they knew I was right, especially after I told them what I had just learned about EB and all of that.

I slept like a log that night. My dreams were consumed with the events of the day. I had nightmares of the *Eaties* logo chasing me through the MECHS snack bar with greasy French fries. It taunted me with an evil laugh, "Eat! Eat!" I defended myself by pummeling it with apple bombs and banana boomerangs. These were some of the strangest dreams I ever had.

The week passed quickly at MECHS. Jessie and I continued to work in the Flyer simulator. Dee went on collecting data from Fred. Berto and Elena kept analyzing patient data from hospitals. Gunderson worked around the clock meeting government officials and consulting with other scientists.

The number of sick was increasing but we had no new insight. Before we left for the weekend I reviewed my goals and set new ones for the following week.

I stood on the Vitascan and Elena downloaded my data. "Congratulations kid. You made an 85 on your goal review," she said.

I was hoping for a hundred. Oh, well. There was always next week. I knew what went wrong. Time got away from me and I just forgot to eat an apple every day. I wasn't gonna beat myself up for it. That never does any good.

"Well, what to you want to add for next week?" Elena asked.

I decide to add a portion of lettuce and tomatoes to my sandwiches. Salads were good and all, but I still liked bread. The MECHS manual said that no foods were bad. Everything in moderation was the key. So was making choices that gave you energy without slowing you down.

Berto patted me on the back. "I'm going to the community center over the weekend if you want to join me. We'll have to start working on your PA—which means physical activity—pretty soon. We might as well get a jump start."

I thanked him for the invitation and told him I would try to meet him if I could. I waited for the others so we could head out together. Jessie took one last look at Fred. Elena checked the cables.

Dee put his arm around Jessie and coaxed her toward the door. "Come on, girl. He's doing fine. The weekend crew will take good care of him. Stay out of here for a couple of days. You need some time off."

The door to the lab opened. We were just walking down the hall when an alarm from the MECHS lab went off. We ran back. The meter above

Fred's hydrotank was flashing CRITICAL. I could see through his helmet that Fred was turning blue. We all looked at each other in awkward silence. None of us knew what to do. We needed Gunderson, and we needed him now. But Gunderson was nowhere to be found.

Voyage

"Code blue hardware section. Code blue!" Jessie was talking to the MECHS communications center through her Vitalink. The CRITICAL light above Fred kept flashing. Some technicians from the lab next door rushed in but they seemed as clueless as we were for what to do. Elena started checking out the hydrotank system. Berto and Dee went through Fred's data on the Vitascan computer. Jessie went looking for Dr. Gunderson.

Suddenly, from the middle of the lab, came a loud BOOM and a ball of light. Sparks flew everywhere. I ducked under a table and covered my head. I was shaking all over. Next came crackling sounds followed by a hydraulic hiss. I made the tactical decision to stay under the table until someone told me otherwise. A million things were happening at once around here. I didn't feel like getting caught in some crossfire.

Then I heard Gunderson's voice. "Elena! Get on the Vitascan. Hurry!" I couldn't see what was going on, but I could imagine. I guessed Gunderson was going to copy Elena's energy to Fred.

"It's not enough," Gunderson said. "Jessie, trade places with Elena!"

About 15 seconds later, the alarm went off. I uncovered my eyes but stayed under the table. By the tone of Jessie's voice, I could tell she was not happy.

"Elena, what's the deal?" Jessie wasn't asking a question. She was demanding an answer.

"I'm sorry. I'll do better next time." Elena was clearly shaken.

All I could see were feet. Jessie bent down and picked up something poking out of Elena's backpack.

"What's this, Elena?"

It was a bag of super-sized corn chips. I got out from underneath the table as Jessie handed me the bag.

"Wings, use your Vitalink to run an analysis on these chips." I emerged from under the table and did as instructed. A list of ingredients appeared on my PDA as I scanned the bag. Jessie ripped the Vitalink out of my hand and practically shoved it up Elena's nose.

Elena tried to explain. "I... um... I thought corn chips could serve as a vegetable."

"Huh? Look how far down corn is on the list. There's almost none in here. You can't keep eating like this. Fred's life depends on us maintaining EB. You know better, Elena. A small bag is enough. If it were me, I wouldn't eat these chips at all. But if you're gonna eat 'em, eat a reasonable portion. Please, I don't want to lose Fred."

"I don't want to lose him either. I'm sorry, Jessie."

Gunderson walked over and put his arms on Jessie and Elena's shoulders. "That was a close call everyone. I hope this helps you understand how important it is for everyone to adhere to the MECHS model for maintaining energy balance. I suggest everyone review it over the weekend. Now, go home and get some rest. Don't worry about Fred. He's re-stabilized, and I will be working in the MECHS lab over the weekend. He won't be alone. I'll see you Monday."

On the way out Elena threw her bag of chips in the trash. I wasn't looking where I was going and ran into something. It knocked me flat on my butt. In front of me was a large silver object perched on the landing pad. At first I didn't get it. Then I realized what I was looking at. It was the Flyer! I had seen pictures of her before. Now, there she was in all her glory, the most versatile flying craft in the world. Wow! Her landing must have been what caused the loud boom. Dr. Gunderson probably flew her in. But how did he get the Flyer get inside the lab?

"Come on Wings," Elena said helping me get back up. "Time to go home. And close your mouth please. I can see your tonsils."

I couldn't take my eyes off the Flyer. Elena had to drag me out of the lab by my shirtsleeve while I gazed at the ship.

Elena and I took the same tram back home. She was mostly silent during the trip. You could tell she was replaying in her head most of what had just happened, or didn't happen, back in the lab. I let her have her peace.

Most towns and cities around the country back then had trams like these. They were clean, efficient, fast and went practically anywhere you could ever want to go. I kind of miss them.

I was still trying to figure out how the Flyer and Gunderson got into the lab when Elena pulled me aside in the car.

"The MARS is top secret you know." Elena's voice was barely audible.

"The what?"

"The Molecular Atomic Reducing System... the M.A.R.S." Elena continued to whisper. "Dr. Gunderson found a way to shrink anything, and anybody for that matter, to micro size. The Flyer can get in and out of MECHS through a small hose connected to the outside of the building. Gunderson went micro and flew the Flyer to the White House for the meeting with the President. There's another MARS at the White House to magnify back to full scale. When you're micro size, it's like being invisible. Way too small to be seen by anyone. We've been experimenting with... hey! What tram station is yours?"

The tram was coming up on my station but I was still in daze. Anything can now be shrunk to the size of a microbe? Even the size of a nano particle? That is just too amazing.

"The next stop is mine," I said.

"Mine too!" Elena said, smiling for the first time in miles. "I didn't know you lived in my neighborhood."

"Well, I didn't know you lived in mine," I said.

"You want to come to my house and hang out for a while? Mom makes a great dinner."

We called our mothers on our Vitalinks and got the necessary approvals. When we got to Elena's, she took me straight into her living room. "Come on, I want to show you something." She used her Vitalink as a remote control. A big flat panel vid screen descended from the ceiling. "See? Big screen LEDGE! Too cool, isn't it? Berto may be good with numbers, but I can rig upanything! What's your thing?"

"Science," I said. "I like to look at the world through science, biology and chemistry mostly. I like thinking about living organisms and molecular systems. It's like... your body is mostly water right? Water is nothing but hydrogen and oxygen molecules stuck together. Molecules are made of atoms and atoms are made up of subatomic particles. Where

62

does it end? We don't know. Maybe you and Berto can build a machine that will take us to the beginning of it all." I hoped I hadn't sounded too geeky.

"We'll go to work on it as soon as we get through this crisis," Elena joked.

I laughed too. It was the first time we had connected in a friendly way. I mean everyone had been nice up to then, but this was like friends hanging out together. It felt good. We played LEDGE for about an hour. She was way ahead of me by the time we quit.

Elena's mom called us to the dinner table. "So, you guys at MECHS know anything about the nanobots the president was talking about? I've heard ambulances running up and down our street all day."

Elena looked at me before answering. "Yes... sort of. They got into Fred. He's in a hydrotank right now. Dr. Gunderson's doing everything he can."

"Oh my! Poor Fred," Mrs. Sanchez said. Then her eyes widened. "But are you and..."

Elena jumped in. "We're fine, all of us. They only got Fred for some reason. I'm sure Dr. Gunderson will figure it out."

Mrs. Sanchez was only somewhat reassured. Turning her mind to dinner seemed to calm her nerves. She had prepared mashed potatoes, biscuits, and macaroni and cheese. In case I turned out to be a picky eater, she also had meatloaf. Ms. Sanchez added brownies for dessert.

Everything looked so good—too good. It was way too much food, and I didn't see a fruit or vegetable in sight. Nothing green, red, orange or yellow... zilch. I didn't want to be rude, but I knew this wasn't exactly the MECHS dietary model Gunderson was talking about.

Elena pulled me close and whispered in my ear when her mother went into the kitchen to answer the phone. "What are we gonna do, Wings? After today, it doesn't seem right to eat as much as I usually do. My mother works hard you know, making dinner. I can't tell her we can't eat it."

I felt bad for Elena. I suggested we get out our Vitalinks and run the energy balance program along with a food substitution routine to see what we could come up with. Maybe if her mom could see the hard data, we could come up with some sort of compromise. I was sure her mom wanted her to be successful with her training goals.

Elena agreed. "I know she wants the best for me. It's just that I haven't really told her what I need to eat to comply with the MECHS model. I grew up on fast food, things that were easy for a single mom working two jobs. I don't want to make things any harder for her."

We ran the portion sizing and EB programs. If we ate a half portion of the mashed potatoes, substituted salad for the mac-n'cheese, and ate fruit instead of brownies, we would do all right. We were busy calculating when her mom came back into the kitchen. "What's the matter? Something wrong with the food?"

"Um, no Mom. It looks great. It's just that..."

Elena explained our dilemma. Her mom was very understanding. She didn't have any fresh fruit but she had some frozen fruit that would make great fruit smoothies. We looked it up on my Vitalink. Six ounces of fruit smoothie was the same calories as a portion of fruit. It looked like that would work. We ran the EB again. If we walked for an hour after dinner we could get close to EB for the day. Sounded like we had a plan.

After dinner Elena's mom gave us some money to buy fruit and salad fixings for the weekend.

We live in what you could call a culturally diverse neighborhood. Elena and I walked to the Spanish market down the street. She bought lettuce, carrots, beets, and something called jicama, though she pronounced he-ka-ma.

"Know what this is?" she asked, holding it up.

I grabbed one of the other veggies and answered, "beets me." Elena winced.

I had never seen a jicama before. It was like a cross between a potato and a pear. The shopkeeper gave us a sample dipped in hummus, and it was delicious. I knew about hummus because my mom bought it all the time at the Middle Eastern market near our house. Hummus was made from chickpeas, but it looked like peanut butter. I never really thought of it before then, but there was sure a lot of variety of food in this part of town.

We said goodbye after shopping and went our separate ways. Elena gave me a jicama to take home. I thanked her for a fun evening and headed down the street. One the way, I noticed how the neighborhood had changed. There was tension in the air that wasn't there the week before. There was a steady stream of sirens in the distance. Mothers walked through streets holding babies close to their chest, as if they were trying to protect them from something. Shop owners who usually sat on sidewalks talking to one another were holed up inside their stores with their doors closed. I think they were afraid that something might sneak in if they kept the door open. People were afraid.

I wanted to tell them that it was going to be all right, that Dr. Gunderson was taking care of everything. I wanted to tell them that I was on the team that was going to save them. But I couldn't. I didn't know anything for sure. I went home and fell asleep with my clothes on. Dreams haunted me again.

Chaos in the streets. People panicking everywhere. Fires burning. People sleeping in alleyways, tired and hungry. The owner from the Spanish market was huddled around a garbage can fire, crying. "Help us! Please!" He held someone wrapped in a dirty blanket but the face was hidden.

There I was, staring at them, dressed in a pristine MECHS flight suit saying, "Trust me. Everything's gonna be okay. I promise." I kept repeating the words over an over like a damaged audio file. My body got hot. I felt like I was on fire. My feet began to melt like hot wax. "Don't' worry. We are going to save you." I melted to the ground like the wicked witch in the Wizard of Oz.

The storeowner took my flight suit and burned it in the fire. He stared into the fire and said, "Liar." Then he fell dead in the street.

Swarms of nanobots ate away at his body from the inside out. In seconds he was gone.

A terrified scream erupted from the blanket, "Noooooooo!" A young woman in ragged clothes with a torn MECHS emblem on her left shoulder emerged. It was Elena! The bots attacked her. She fell to the ground and disappears in a nanosecond. Minutes later the entire planet was consumed by fire. It exploded into tiny particles like a dandelion in the wind. The planet was destroyed, turned back into the parts of its sum. It was the Big Bang in small scale.

I stayed in bed the next morning looking at the ceiling. The phone rang. It was Berto. He had been having weird dreams too. He suggested we meet at the community center and play basketball or something. For Berto, exercise was the sure cure for everything. I told him I'd meet him after I took a shower.

I caught the tram and was on my way. Most everyone used the tram. It was much better for the environment than any other mode of transportation, except walking or bicycling. There was no smog because the tram didn't run on gasoline. It was powered by a combination of water and nuclear fusion. Somehow the power made water travel super fast through the system. The force of the water propelled gears that moved the tram forward. It was sort of like being powered by a water wheel except the tram system could run up to one hundred times faster than a water wheel. It was a perfect marriage between old and new technology.

I was starving by the time I got to the community center. I had forgotten about breakfast before I left. I asked Berto where I could get something to eat. We walked to a smoothie joint. I was starting to like smoothies. Berto called them "healthy snacks." He ordered me a smoothie with protein powder, strawberries, bananas and pineapple. I chose 100% apple juice for the base. I wondered if I could make something like that at home. We had a blender. I didn't really need the protein powder. I could use milk or yogurt instead. Mom never bought us yogurt before, but then again, Dad and I never asked her to.

"Come on, Berto. Let's see what you're made of." Was that me talking? I guess the smoothie went to my head. I wasn't a very good basketball player, but I felt good enough to take on Berto in a little one-on-one.

We played to ten points. I lost. It was the fastest game of one-on-one I ever played. He beat me so bad, but I didn't care. It was a lot of fun, and it felt good to exercise.

The weekend was over before I knew it. I had just entered the MECHS lab when that same boom and bright light hit. This time I saw what it was. The Flyer was enlarging on the MARS platform. It just appeared out of nowhere. The canopy opened and out popped Jessie.

"Whoa! That was a trip! Hey, Wings. You're up next."

70

I had no idea what she was talking about. Gunderson gathered the team and went over the plan for the week. I finally found out the complete story of the hush-hush project. Gunderson was taking miniaturization exploration to a whole new level. No more construction at a micro scale. He had engineered a system that could shrink full-sized objects to nano size. He could reverse the process as well. That's how he planned to make a new series of nanobots, the most sophisticated bots ever produced.

Gunderson had decided to use the MARS to shrink the Flyer and send it into Fred to capture one of the rogue nanobots. Bringing it back to the lab for dissection would reveal what went wrong. From there, finding a solution should be easy. Jessie and I would be the pilots for the mission.

The whole idea struck me as either brilliant or crazy. Shrink the Flyer down to the size of blood cell and voyage inside the human body? That was just too fantastic. I knew Gunderson was a genius, but for the first time I thought he might be a genius turning mad scientist. You know, there are such people. They're not just in movies and computer games. They start out as Einsteins and then, something snaps. They begin thinking they can defy the very scientific principles that made them famous. I sure hoped Dr. Gunderson wasn't teetering on that narrow ledge.

Jessie and I worked the Flyer simulator all week. I also started training inside a pressurized miniaturization simulator. My body had to get used to being shrunk and then blown back up. It was similar to what deep-sea divers do to avoid getting the bends. Reduction to micro scale really stresses the body. We had to stay in shape.

I went home and crashed again at the end of the day. I was exhausted. I think I ate some fruit before I passed out. Mom got a little worried when she saw me too tired to sit up and eat a full dinner. She was getting used to this but didn't think the pace was doing my health much good.

When I got to the lab the next morning Gunderson called an early meeting. He told me to get my goal review and goal setting out of the way first thing. He had scheduled a Flyer test run after lunch and said we should report to the MARS platform dressed in flight suits at 1300 hours.

Dee helped me with my goal review. I did okay but not great. I managed to add a portion of lettuce and tomatoes only fifty percent of the time. We looked closely at what happened and discovered that it all boiled down to time, availability and just plain forgetting.

When I was home, I couldn't take the time to slice tomatoes or wash the lettuce. It was easier to make a sandwich and run. When I was willing to take the time to slice tomatoes and clean lettuce, I often found that we didn't have any because I had forgotten to ask Mom to buy some. If I ate lunch at the MECHS snack bar I would often forget to add the tomatoes and lettuce. Maintaining EB was not simple. It was easier to push it back on the priority list. As I later found out, I may have had my priorities wrong.

Dee helped me think of ways to reach my target goals. I could slice tomatoes and clean lettuce ahead of time so that when I made a sandwich it would be easy to put it together. I could leave a note asking Mom to remember to get lettuce and tomatoes, or we could have a weekly checklist that we kept on the fridge. When I was at MECHS, I could ask other team members to remind me to add lettuce and tomatoes to my sandwich. There are lots of ways to skin a cat; I mean peel a tomato... whatever.

Just like previous weeks, I needed to add new goals while keeping up with goals I had already set. I decided my goal for the week would be working out a system with the person in my house who bought the groceries and prepared the food. Most of the time, that was Mom. Dad helped out occasionally. Sometimes he would grill hamburgers and hot dogs on weekends. Maybe we could try grilling chicken or vegetables for a change. I thought the list idea was a good way to help Mom remember to keep fruit and vegetables around the house.

So far, I had added one apple or another kind of fruit a day, one serving of lettuce and tomatoes to my sandwiches, and now I was trying to find ways to get support at home. It was hard to do all this alone, but hey, if you don't get the ball rolling, who will?

"Come on. Let's get some lunch," Dee said.

"You're gonna need energy for the test flight, Wings, but I'd keep it on the light side if I were you. Know what I mean jelly bean?"

I knew exactly what he meant. I remember reading about the way the first astronauts used to train almost a hundred years ago. They would fly in this plane that took steep climbs and sharp dives to create a sense of weightlessness. This would prepare their bodies to live in zero gravity in outer space. They called their plane the "vomit comet." Weird flying can really turn your stomach inside out and upside down.

Dee and I went to the snack bar for some fruit. Then we headed back to the lab. Dee, God bless him, was the oddest one on the team. That may be why I enjoyed him the most. He was the first person I had ever met with psychic abilities. I mean, I had seen fortunetellers at the circus and "professionals" with their own shops, but I always thought they were fake. Dee was different. One day when we were alone in the lab, Berto told me the whole clairvoyant thing with Dee was hogwash. I didn't tell him that I was convinced Dee was the genuine article.

When we got back to the lab I got into my flight suit and went over a few details with Jessie. I walked over to Fred just before we climbed into the cockpit. I put my hand on the hydrotank like I was asking for his blessing. He's a pilot, I'm a pilot. Pilots have a special kind of regard for each other, even if they had never actually worked together. Fred just floated in the tank, asleep. For a second, I thought I could feel him acknowledge my presence. Or, maybe I was hallucinating. Not enough sleep; yeah that was probably it.

Dr. Gunderson assembled the team. Jessie and I strapped into the Flyer. Elena watched the pressure controls. Dee monitored Fred. Berto manned the communications console.

"Flyer maiden infusion voyage ready to go," Gunderson said. "Look smart everyone."

"Elena," Berto said standing at his console, "I hope the Flyer is ready for this."

"I have some issues with the gyros. The machine shop still hasn't finished the new ones, but they promised these would hold. Let's just keep this short and sweet."

Jessie chimed in over the communications link. "We do have aqua maneuvering control, don't we?"

"No fancy moves for now," Elena advised. "Keep it simple."

Jessie smiled at me. "Well, we can always bang on the right side of the dash if the gyros cut out again. That usually brings them back."

I thought Jessie was kidding but Elena heard the remark. Elena was in one her serious moods. "Yeah, that would be fine on a run through a test tube in the lab, but I wouldn't want to try it in vivo."

"You ready, Wings?" Jessie asked.

No, I wasn't ready, but I gave her the thumbs up anyway. I pressed the hydraulic control that closed the cockpit canopy. In less than thirty seconds we were sealed inside an airtight container, like peanuts in a tin can.

There I was, in the Flyer, preparing for the first mission of its kind in the entire world. This was like those who traveled far into space or deep into the center of the earth. I would be voyaging into a human body. It was an indescribable feeling.

Everything was just as we had rehearsed. The Flyer simulator was an exact replica of the real thing. During the countdown we would undergo molecular reduction. If successful we would shoot into the transport tube connecting the MARS to the hydrotank. The ship's computers would automatically fly us into Fred's body.

Dr. Gunderson came over the radio, "Okay everyone, let's go micro. Prepare for reduction. Everything looks good from here. Engaging the MARS..."

Berto was in charge of the countdown, "Ten, nine..." With each tick the Flyer shook faster and faster. Control lights in the cockpit flashed off and on. I dug my nails into the armrests. What am I doing here? "Seven, six..."

My heart and spine were being pulled to the back of my seat like a marble in a slingshot, tighter and tighter.

"Three, two, one..."

I thought I would snap in two from the pressure.

"Reduction complete."

The slingshot released. It felt like we were twisting and turning and tumbling and crashing all at the same time. The motion was wild and unpredictable. We were constantly being thrown in one direction and then the next. This was totally unlike flying a plane, I thought. It felt like my skin was being stretched to the point where it would be torn away from the muscle and bone.

Fortunately the centrifugal force kept me glued to the seat.

"Oh, man! What's haaa...peeen..iiiing?" I thought it was Jessie shouting, but it may have been me. Outside was swirling. Every warning light in the cockpit was flashing. Alarms were ringing all over the place.

"Abort mission!" It was Gunderson on the radio. "Abort mission! Jessie? Do you read me? ABORT THE MISSION!"

Jessie tried to reach the abort button but the violent force of the gyrations held back her hand. She tried again and again to reach it, but couldn't. I released my hand from the armrest and grabbed onto hers. Together we pushed our way through the invisible forces until we reached the abort panel. We pushed the abort sequence button several times but nothing happened.

The warning system announced, "Abort malfunction. Abort malfunction."

Gunderson voice was frantic, "Abort! Jessie!

" Abort the miss..." Communications went silent.

Jessie tried radioing back. "Dr. Gunderson! Come in Dr. Gunderson!"

Nothing. Another alarm warned the data link was down. We were now on our own, spiraling out of control somewhere inside Fred's body. I tried to let go of my fear, but I was too afraid. I really gotta find myself a new mental shelf, I thought.

Things slowed down enough to where I could finally keep my head in one place. I looked over at Jessie. She looked calm but very concerned. I knew that if she was concerned, we should probably prepare for the worst.

Jessie looked at me and grinned. "No worries, Wings. We'll have this sorted out in just a..."

Darkness. The Flyer's power went out. We started spinning faster and faster again. It felt like we were lost in some endless black hole. There was a violent jolt to the right and Jessie was thrown against the canopy. She slumped down in her flight chair. I tried to reach her but couldn't. My energy level was being quickly depleted. Every thought I ever had in my life was racing through my mind. Distorted mini movies of key life events randomly flashed by until there was nothing but black. Black followed by nothing. I felt the last bit of energy drain from my body until all was gone. So this is what dying feels like.

Then, nothing.

Specimen

The Flyer came to a sudden stop. The cockpit lights came on as I regained consciousness. Jessie was still out but the maneuvering controls were back online. I took the yoke and slowly moved the Flyer forward. I don't know why, but I took a few pictures of our surroundings. There wasn't much to see. It looked like we were in a dark cave. At this point, I didn't know if we were in Fred or inside the transport tube.

Everything was quiet, eerily quiet. Then I heard someone trying to communicate, followed by a lot of static.

"Wings come in. Wings, do you read me?"

"Yes, Dr. Gunderson. I hear you."

"Is everything alright?" he asked.

I shook Jessie. "Jessie! Jessie! It's Dr. Gunderson."

She slowly came to. "What happened?"

"You passed out. So did I."

"We seem to be in one piece," she said into her microphone, groggily. "It looks like the backup systems kicked in."

Elena responded, "Actually, it's the backup of the backup. What's your status?"

Jessie continued her assessment. "Life support is good. The hull seems to be intact. I read a few mechanical systems offline. My head hurts."

"Can you plot a course back to the extraction point?" Elena sounded worried.

"Nope, the navigation computer is offline. So are the gyros." Jessie hit the dashboard on the side. "Still no gyros. Looks like you get to say 'I told you so,' Elena." Jessie was trying to keep it light. Elena was not amused.

I noticed a large mass on the Flyer's scanner. I pointed to the screen and called to Jessie. "Look! Is that what I think it is?"

"Yeah." Jessie reached for controls, but her hand slid off. She was sweating and still groggy from the bang on her head. "You're gonna have to catch one, Wings. I can't do it."

Dee came on the radio, "Jessie and Wings, I'm monitoring your bio data and heart rates just went right through the roof, especially yours Jessie. Are you two okay?"

"We've got bots, Dee," Jessie said. "They're all over the ship."

Just outside the canopy were hundreds of nanobots in all shapes, sizes and colors. The ones closest to us looked like spiders, in fact, just like the model in the MECHS lab. Jessie was turning pale. Dee tried to calm her down, "It's okay Jessie. Take it easy. These are robots, not spiders. Do the biofeedback like we practiced."

Jessie closed her eyes and started taking deep, slow breaths. Dee continued talking to her. I was surprised at her reaction. It wasn't exactly fear. It was, well, something else. Kinda hard to describe.

"You're gonna have to try and nab one of those bots, Wings." Dr. Gunderson gave me instructions on using the claw. "Also, while we work up a way to get you guys out, get some pictures of the bots around the ship," he said.

I took about a dozen more photographs and then turned my attention to catching a bot. I flipped on the searchlights. Most of the swarm moved away from the Flyer. Twenty or thirty stayed close. Some were in front, others were directly above us. All I needed was one. The claw was a device used for collecting samples during missions. I figured I could just thrust the claw into the middle of the cluster of bots in front and start grabbing. Of course, I was wrong. The minute I went for it the Flyer started rocking and rolling again. The lights started flickering as the Flyer started spinning. I had absolutely no control over the ship. We were doing three-sixties when I blacked out again.

The next thing I knew, the canopy was open and I was staring up at Berto. "Have an nice trip, Wings?"

"Wonderful, thank you, Berto. And how was your day?"

Berto grabbed my arm and pulled me up. "It was swell," he said. "You two are extremely lucky, you know. That swarm of bots literally pushed you to the extraction point."

"They what?" Jessie was groggy but awake.

Dee appeared and helped Jessie out of the Flyer. She was still rattled.

Dr. Gunderson asked us to get on the Vitascan so he could check our post-flight status. Everything checked out. Jessie was bruised but okay. My body was a little stressed and I was a little low in the energy department, but that was to be expected. He suggested I double up on my goals for the next week. He suggested I set a new goal every three days instead of once a week. The faster I got in tiptop shape, the less stress I would experience on missions.

I had already set a goal to ask my mom and dad to keep healthy foods in the house. Dr. Gunderson suggested I add a couple of glasses of water to my goals. My energy profile revealed that I had not been drinking enough of the right fluids. I mostly drank sodas and fruit drinks. Gunderson told me most fruit drinks don't have much fruit in them at all. They are made out of water, sugar and a little fruit flavoring. Those don't do us much good. Pure water was better. Our bodies need water to function properly. Humans are like sponges; with no water we become dry and brittle.

I added two glasses of water a day to my goals for the week. That would complete the first phase of the MECHS nutrition and physical activity program. After I reviewed my success with these goals I would move on to Physical Activity, the PA segment of the program.

"Hey! Check it out." Elena called out from under the Flyer.

Berto and I went to see what was up. I looked under the Flyer. You won't believe what we found. It was a nanobot, and it was clutching to the underside of a wing.

"Looks like a bot hitched a ride," Elena said. "It went through the quantum magnification field with you guys. Anyone want to try to pull it off?"

"I'll do it." I got a portable claw and tried to pry the bot off the vent. I pulled so hard that I landed on the floor. Our bot didn't like beingpoked at because when I tried to yank on it a second time, it freed itself and started flying around the lab. It was emitting high frequency tones, *schwee—peep—be—ba—da—beep—beep—beep*, as it zoomed around us.

Dee ran in. "Don't hurt it!"

Yeah, right. Who was he kidding? That thing was dangerous. The bot was careening around the lab, diving at us, bouncing off walls and then disappearing behind equipment.

"It's trying to communicate," Dee shouted.

"You mean it's trying to kill us!" Berto said attempting to bring Dee back to reality.

Dee grabbed a blanket. I kept chasing the bot with the claw. Berto and Elena tried to corner the thing. We jumped over and under tables. We ran into and fell over each other. We must have looked ridiculous. If bots could laugh, this one should be slapping its six knees.

We finally trapped it in one corner of the lab. I went to claw it but Dee jumped in front of the pole, tripping me in the process. I fell tumbling to the ground. Berto and Elena fell on top of me. The claw went straight up into the air. Then Dee tripped over the blanket and also fell to the ground. It must have been divine intervention because the moment I reached up, the bot ran smack into the claw. I quickly clamped it shut and tried to hold it down. It was a strong sucker.

Gunderson and Jessie ran in just as we snagged the bot. "Get up off that floor," Jessie said. "What's the matter with you guys? Not getting enough sleep?"

"We got us a bot!" I was probably screaming.

Gunderson helped us drag it to a table where he strapped it down. Order returned to the lab, for a moment anyway. Soon, Dee and Berto were arguing about the "botspeak."

"That's not a signal," Berto said. "It's random noise. Maybe its static filter has gone out."

"It's language, Berto," Dee said. We just don't understand it."

"You're nuts, Dee!" Berto was angry. "This is a nanobot, a machine. Machines don't talk. Dr. Gunderson, did you program the bots to talk?

"Well, not exactly talk..."

"See? End of discussion, Dee."

Gunderson told Berto and Dee to knock it off. He then instructed Berto and Elena to finish checking out the Flyer's mechanical and computer systems. With Berto occupied near the MARS, Gunderson quietly took Dee aside and asked him to follow his intuition about the bot. "I don't know what that sound is, but it's very intriguing. Let me know what you come up with Dee," Gunderson said.

Jessie and I were sent to the LifePad to recoup. Gunderson asked us to stay at MECHS over the weekend for observation. That would eventually become standard operating procedure for new program missions. The effects of the Molecular Anatomy Reducer were not completely known back then. Quantum magnification field theory was in its infancy. Thinking back on it, it's mind boggling to know that I had been shrunk down to the size of a blood cell and then enlarged, all in a matter of minutes—and nobody fully understood how the process worked!

The LifePad was equipped with a sound system, some exercise equipment, a couple of cots and three or four food vending units. The food units had almost anything you could ever want to eat. I particularly liked the variety of waters you could get from all over the world. In case you were real particular, the food units were also connected to the net.

Jessie relaxed in a floating massage chair listening to music. I sat in a beanbag and played a little LEDGE. I was still too wound up to nap. The mineral water was a new experience for me. It didn't taste special, more like regular water except a little heavier. I figured that since my palate didn't find it too special, I would have to get my mind involved with helping me like the stuff. I also had to make a real effort to tell myself how good water was for me. I had done it before with math. I hated math in the beginning, but you can't do science without math. So I learned math and soon learned to like math.

I eventually fell asleep. And, for the first time since I joined the team, I slept like a baby. It was Dee who woke me up. "You guys must be hungry. I brought you some soup, crackers and fruit."

The three of us ate. Dee had a worried look on his face. Something was bothering him.

"What's wrong?" I asked.

"Look, sorry about the bot incident back there. I just couldn't let you hurt it with those industrial forceps."

"No problem, Dee," I said. "I don't have much experience around nanobots anyway."

"None of us do," Jessie chimed in. "Not these kinds of bots, anyway. I'm just glad that thing didn't hurt anyone.

90

Berto and Elena entered with news that the Flyer was in good shape, considering. We hadn't gotten very far in Fred's body, but for the distance traveled, we did well. I wasn't exactly sure where we wound up once we left the transport tube.

Berto stroked his chin and said, "Well according to the playback log, you made it to the opening of Fred's throat."

"That's as far as we got?" I said.

Jessie turned to me and her eyes went wide. It was all coming back to her. "I'm sorry I freaked out on you, Wings. You were great. I don't know what happened to me."

"We both did fine," I said. My attempt at consoling her didn't work. Jessie, as usual, was being hard on herself. For someone like Jessie, there was either success or failure. There was nothing in between. "You know, we did get the bot we came for.

"Yeah, completely by accident," Jessie said.

Gunderson came into the LifePad. "I'll take mission accomplished any way it comes. Now, if you don't mind, I want to read your energy profiles before you do too much else."

We went back to the Vitascan. "It looks like you both have negative readouts," Dee noted. "Your output is a lot more than your intake. I guess that means that molecular anatomy reduction and quantum magnification really burn calories."

"So does that mean we can eat more than crackers and soup?" At that point, I was starving.

"Okay, eat some real food," Gunderson said. "But I don't want you two going out right now. Stay in the MECHS lab."

Berto suggested we surf up some menus on the net and order online through the food units. "They'll deliver it right to us," he told me.

I had never thought of ordering online before. Berto had written a program that could sync up with online menus to help us practice nutrition goals. He called it his "EB Simulator." I could play with substituting menu items, check portion sizing, add water, and look at the ingredients of food and drink items. Who would have ever thought that hamburger buns had sugar in them? I checked out Mexican food, burger joints, chicken, fish and Chinese takeout. I ordered a fajita salad from Macho's, a local Mexican drive thru.

After we ate, Dee checked my EB again. I was surprised to find out that I had room for a little dessert. I got some ice cream from the snack bar in the LifePad, double chocolate nut fudge. Looks like the MARS had some good side effects. Who cares if you get shrunk down to the size of a microbe and shot through a tube so long as there's an ice cream sundae waiting for you at the other end?

Gunderson called the team together for a brief meeting. He told the others to come back Saturday and prepare to work a long day. But, he told Jessie and me to get back to the LifePad and get some sleep.

We were at work again at the crack of dawn. Dee was playing with a recording of botspeak. Berto called it "bot squeak," and he didn't much like it. Dee may be clairvoyant, but I had to agree with Berto. These couldn't be real signals. If the bots could talk, we would be dealing with a whole new can of worms. Talking robots? No, not just talking, thinking nanobots! Something can't talk unless it thinks of something to say. Thinking, talking bots? That was way beyond the realm of possibility. I mean, we're not talking science fiction here.

Elena worked with Jessie on the Flyer's stabilizers. For obvious reasons, Jessie wanted a smoother ride next time out. Berto and I helped Gunderson run tests on the bot. Gunderson powered the bot down to shut it up for a while. Every time someone would go near it, the bot would go crazy with botspeak, so he had no choice. He put it into sleep mode.

We looked deep inside the bot's core programs. We took readings from various parts of bot systems. We took photos of its insides with a fiber optic camera. By the end of the day we had collected a huge amount of data. Tomorrow, we would start processing our findings.

Dr. Gunderson was pleased with our progress. He dismissed the team for the evening. The others went home while Jessie and I stayed in the lab. We made up our bunks and hit the memory foam. I read a few pages in the MECHS manual. Jessie listened to a hypnosis tape Dee said would help her get over arachnophobia.

As I fell asleep I could hear tiny oxygen bubbles popping on the surface of the hydrotank. For a minute I fantasized the bots in Fred escaping from the

94

tank to rescue their captured comrade. As I drifted off I found myself battling an army of bots. It was a very powerful dream.

Jessie woke me up in the middle of the night.

She also had dreams about bots. The bots had captured her. It really shook her up. I made her a cup of green tea, and we sat up talking for a while. We didn't discuss MECHS stuff. We talked about life.

My mom called first thing the following morning. She asked me what she should pick up at the store. She wanted to make sure I had everything I needed when I got home that evening. I emailed her a list, then I took a moment to review my goals regarding asking and negotiating for what I needed. Finally, a perfect score. I felt really good about that. I like doing things one hundred percent.

It took three or four days for Berto and me to put the data together. We methodically hashed through tons of previous bot design and configuration files. Looking at the bot on the lab table through a holographic scanner, you could see it had most of the characteristics of the current 200 series. If you more looked closely however, you could see some significant changes had been made. For one, it had been modified to withstand the rigors of surviving inside the human body. It emitted special signals that effectively made it invisible to antibodies. Our body defense systems would never pick it up. There were also significant differences in its core programming. It wasn't clear what these differences meant. We looked for the missing link for hours until we finally gave up. We called in Gunderson who took one look at the code and said, "207."

What? It sounded familiar but I couldn't remember where I heard it before.

Jessie was working on the Flyer when Gunderson called out the number. "What did you just say, sir?"

"I said 207. It's from an experiment I was running last week. The 207 is a new kind of nanobot; a medical nanobot. It's a 200 series designed to survive in the bloodstream." He pulled a flask off the shelf with a label that read MEDIBOT EXPERIMENT #207. He pointed to the bot, then to the flask, then to Fred. "But how did it get from here to there?"

We all froze. Gunderson kept looking at the flask. I looked at Jessie who was just about to say something when the videophone went off. It was the president.

96

"Hello Earl," she said looking at us over Dr. Gunderson's shoulder.

"Madame President, it's good to see you."

"Hello to all of you too."

There was a long awkward pause as we stood there waiting for her to continue. "I'm afraid I've got bad news, Earl."

"How bad?" Gunderson asked.

"End of the world bad," she said.

Gunderson thought for a moment before answering. "That *is* bad."

Going Global

Just as I was thinking, how could things possibly get any worse?, things got worse. The president showed us news clips of patients and hospitals from all over the world. Doctors from Europe, Russia and Asia were looking at hundreds of bioscans, all showing nanobots swarming through bloodstreams. The situation was no longer confined to the United States. We were dealing with an international problem now.

"Over the last few days," the president said, "other countries did not allow flights from America to land or ships to dock. They quarantined us. Some of our more vocal friends even wanted to nuke us to keep this from spreading."

"Some friends," Berto mumbled.

"While I was explaining to them why nuking wasn't a good idea," the president continued, "reports of nanoinfestations were pouring in from every continent. This has gone global, Earl."

"How is that possible?" Jessie said. "Nanobots would have to move at supersonic speeds to spread around the world that fast."

"Supersonic nanobots?" the president asked.

"Madame President," Gunderson said, "Even supersonic wouldn't spread bots this far in so short a time frame. Something else is going on."

Dee offered a suggestion. "Maybe they're communicating..."

Berto rolled his eyes. Gunderson raised his hand. Dee stopped talking.

Gunderson continued. "All I know for sure, Madame President, is that a new medibot experiment somehow got loose from the MECHS lab. How that happened, I don't know. The medibot was designed to enter and survive inside a human body. We've found it in Fred's bloodstream. What has me more concerned however is that all of the bots you're showing me in these news clips are acting like the medibot, but they are not medibots. Look at this."

Gunderson rewound the clips and pointed to the screen. "These aren't 207s. That's a 47 nanobot. That's a 103. That one is 118. Here is a 56 and a 43. That looks like a 154." Then Gunderson moved his finger to a monitor showing one of Fred's Vitascans. "Here's the swarm inside Fred. I didn't notice it at first but - zoom in on this area will you, Wings." I moved to the console and changed the magnification on the monitor. "There are a few real 207s among them, but they appear to be rare. Here's an old 43, the bot that breaks down hydrocarbon emissions in the air. And that one, that's a 16, probably from the self-cleaning carpet at *Eaties.*" By the time he finished speaking he had named at least a dozen more bots acting like 207s.

"It's my fault, sir." Jessie said.

The president's gaze turned to Jessie as Gunderson spoke. "What are you talking about?" Gunderson asked.

"I opened the flask." She pointed to the flask on Gunderson's workstation.

Gunderson said nothing for moment. Then, "You did what?"

"I'm the one that let the 207s out." She looked at her feet. Jessie's voice was barely audible.

"What were you doing in my work area?"

"We were passing by on our way out. I opened the flask to tease Fred. This is my fault. This is all my fault." Jessie's eyes were pointed toward the floor.

"You know better than to tamper with my work."

"Yes, sir. I..."

Gunderson let out a long sigh. He lowered his head and started speaking softly to her. "You may have let them out, but they shouldn't be behaving like this. They are designed to survive in the bloodstream, but they shouldn't be making anyone sick. "The 207s only attack viruses." He pointed to the pictures on the screen. "And it doesn't explain why all these other bots are in the bloodstream. Their programming does not allow them to enter a human body."

"The 207's programming," Berto asked, "it's designed to evolve, right?"

Gunderson thought for a moment. "Yeah. That's the only way to keep up with Smart Germs." His face was puzzled. "But not these other bots. Their programming is fixed.

"But they are behaving just like 207s," Berto said.

"They must have mutated somehow," Gunderson said. He turned around to face the president again. "But that's impossible. They would have to be reprogrammed."

"Why aren't any of us sick?" I had to ask.

Gunderson now turned to me. "Good point, Wings. I have no idea." With his back to the president he told us, "Go home everyone. You've done some excellent work today. We got our first breakthrough."

"Are you sure you should be sending them home at a time like this, Earl?" The president sounded concerned.

"Working my staff to death isn't going to save the world, Madame President. We've got a good start. I suggest you leave the research to me."

"I hope you know what you're doing. This thing started on American soil. It's our responsibility to fix it."

"And we will fix it," Gunderson said emphatically. The president signed off.

Gunderson's mood had definitely perked up but everyone else was pretty tense. It seemed like we had a revolution on our hands. Like the bots had gotten together and decided to take over the world or something.

The team left the lab for the evening. I think we were as much discouraged as afraid. As I rode the tram home I looked at the faces of those around me. I wondered which one would be next. I wondered if they had any idea what was going on. I wanted to scream, "Run for your lives! Get out while you can." But these were bots we were talking about. They were everywhere. Where could you run?

When I got home I sat on the edge of my bed until one o'clock in the morning. Finally, I decided that whatever was going to happen would happen, like it or not. I might as well go to sleep.

On my way to the lab the next morning Jessie stopped me in the hallway. "Do you know what today is?"

I didn't.

"It's your progress review. Here." She handed me a white legal-size envelope with the Edutrust seal stamped in the middle.

It was time for an interim progress review already? The time had gone by so quickly.

"Come on. You need to go back to the orientation center and answer another questionnaire. I'll go with you."

I read through the Edutrust review on the way down the hall. I had done well. My overall score was a ninety-two, good enough for me to stay in the program.

I did my final goal review for the first four modules. After I reviewed how I was doing with my water intake, Jessie guided me through a new baseline questionnaire. I noticed that there were fewer trainees in the hall this time around, in fact a lot less. I was lucky to be one of the ones that made it this far.

Whereas the first four modules had focused on eating and drinking, the second half would focus on physical activity. I wasn't very consistent with physical activity. I have never been. I exercised in spurts. I knew PA was good for me, just like I knew eating vegetables and fruit was good for me, but I could never make it part of my regular routine.

"You're going to have to start setting PA goals," Jessie said. "Don't worry about it. I'll help you. I've been through the same thing. Most of us science heads don't think about what's going on from the neck down. At MECHS though, you've got to stay in shape, head to toe." Jessie's face suddenly turned very serious. "Probably now more than ever."

She printed out the PA workout sheet the orientation computer prepared for me. During the questionnaire, I had said one of the reasons I didn't exercise was that I spent most of my time inside studying or working. Apparently that was no excuse. The computer made my first goal indoor resistance training. It had to get done.

"Why don't you come over to my place when we get out of here today?" Jessie offered. "We can work on it together."

"Sounds good to me."

The rest of the team was hunched over their workstations when we entered the lab. Fred was still sleeping like a baby. A baby in a flight suit floating in a hydrotank, that is. Gunderson was pouring over the data from the weekend. He held up an image from a European patient. "We need more information on these other bots. We don't know what happened to change their core programming. They're behaving like 207s, but they are not 207s."

"I still think they're communicating with one another," Dee chimed in.

"Yes Dee," Gunderson explained, "all bots communicate, but in a very rudimentary way. That's how masses of bots coordinate their efforts to clean up water and the like."

"I know that, sir. But I think it's more than that. If we can get another bot through the quantum magnification process and put them together and observe them, I might be able to prove my theory."

There was a huge pause in the room. Everyone waited for Gunderson to speak. Berto had a scowl on his face.

Gunderson thought for awhile, then said, "You might be right, son. I think we should give it a try."

Berto stomped off. Dee started repeating some kind of gibberish to himself. *Schwee—peep—be—ba—da—beep—beep—beep*. It sounded like noise to me but to Dee, these were words and sentences. For the first time I thought he just might be right. Maybe this was some kind of language.

"I'm ready go back in, sir," Jessie volunteered. "I don't want to put you through that again, Jessie."

"It's okay, sir. I'll be fine. Besides, I've got Wings."

"That's true. You've got Wings."

Gunderson approved the mission. Jessie and I checked out the Flyer with Elena. Everything was looking pretty good for another reduction. I suggested we work with the simulator for a while. I wanted to practice my wave riding skills a bit more.

That was one of the cooler things about the Flyer, it was so versatile. She was smaller than most ships so she could turn on a dime. She was capable of flying in so many modes. I could turn her sideways or fly upside down. She could skim across an ocean full of crashing waves, dive like a porpoise, and hover like a helicopter. The simulator allowed me to choose from a series of maneuvers. I could work on wave riding, submerging or flying. I could also select Random and the computer would set up an obstacle course with a variety of unpredictable maneuvers. The Random sequence was closer to what you would encounter in a real situation, so I chose that.

"Looking good." Jessie watched me. It was nice. She was nice. I started to see what Fred found

108

attractive in her: simple innocence, amazing talent and stubborn tenacity. But no attitude. Jessie had absolutely no feelings of superiority. I realized how lucky I was to be here. I was starting to have fun.

"Ouch!" That came from behind us, somewhere in the lab.

"What's the matter?" We jumped out of the simulator cockpit to find Berto holding his finger.

"I shocked myself," he said.

"How?" Jessie asked. "What were you doing?"

"I was trying to hook up the Energy Balance Simulator." Berto was on the floor with half of his body inside the access panel of his workstation. "There, that's it. Working now. Want to try it?"

"No. Not really," Jessie said.

"Heck, I'll try it," I volunteered.

Berto explained his new invention. "It's an energy balance simulator called EBSim. Like a lot of programs I've been working on lately, it takes the front end of LEDGE and expands on it. I plan on turning it into a new training module. EBSim can project the effects of your food intake and PA output into the future to show you what your balance would look like. It also shows the energy producing potential of foods, like how many calories or energy it takes to efficiently run your body."

Yet another video game from Berto the Magic Programmer that did more than simply entertain. Berto was also really talented. EBSim showed how your body needs a certain amount of calories to function properly. Berto had even programmed animated help diagrams. One showed how you got calories from the food you ate. There was a little movie of an apple going into a stomach. When the apple mixed with stomach acid, heat energy was released. The heat energy traveled to little animated cells that would use the energy to help repair parts of the body or just keep it functioning properly.

"What do you think?" Berto asked me.

"Not bad," I said. We didn't get halfway through the program before he decided to re-write a few algorithms.

"You can be my first test subject tomorrow. I'll have it finished by then." Berto shut down the simulator and headed toward the door.

"Okay," I said. "See you tomorrow." Tomorrow? I looked up at the clock. Was it really time to go home? The day went by fast.

Jessie and I took the tram to her house. She didn't live far from me, but far enough for me to notice that there was a good amount of room between the houses in her part of town. In my neighborhood, you could see the guy next door taking a shower.

Jessie went to work as soon as we got to her house. "Let's get PA started, Wings."

"I thought you said you had indoor exercise equipment here. Where is it?"

"No equipment needed," she said. "We're doing resistance training. All you need is your body and a few odds and ends from around the house."

"Okay Chief, whatever you say."

We worked five muscle groups: arms, legs, stomach, chest and glutes. We used furniture and walls instead of equipment. I never realized how you could use your own body and common household items to get a real workout. With workouts like this I could have my own fitness club right at home.

At the end of the session I set resistance training goals for the week. I could use the same kinds of things from around my house, I wassure of it. I thanked Jessie for the workout and went home. On the way, I played LEDGE on my Vitalink. I started to think the game was a metaphor for what we were all experiencing. If you think about it, we were thrown into a tight spot and charged with figuring a way out. One move in the wrong direction and the entire world could go plummeting into the abyss. Maybe we are all players in some galactic video game somewhere—a game where players could die and not come back to play again. This was a serious video game, if ever there was one.

I got to the lab a little early the next morning. It was just Fred and me, and Fred didn't look too good. In fact, he was looking a little worse each day. I knew we had to hurry and figure something out or we were going to lose him. I saw the bot on the lab table. The answer had to be inside this thing somewhere.

I replayed the events in my mind. Jessie opened flask 207. Medibots escaped from the flask and jumped into Fred. We went to lunch and some of them must have jumped out of Fred and into people we passed in the street. Those people must have passed the 207s to hundreds of people around the country and then the world. But how did they move around so quickly? The whole thing took less than a couple of days. Did they catch rides on trams, cars, boats and planes? We ran dispersion calculations in the MECHS lab. Trams, cars, boats and planes don't travel fast enough for them to have spread this fast. And why are all these other bots behaving like 207s?

Berto came in and made a beeline for the lab table. Dee soon joined him. They were just looking at the bot when Berto picked up a spanner probe.

"What are you doing, Berto?" Dee asked.

"I'm removing its primary module so I can see what's gone wrong with the programming."

"Please don't do that. You could wipe out all its code."

"Yeah, so?"

"So, I won't be able to access the speech center and continue with my experiment."

"Experiment? You call what you are doing an experiment?" Berto was genuinely angry. "Dee, why can't you get it through your head that bots don't talk!"

"What about the tone patterns?"

"It's a defect somewhere, maybe the audio interface. They're insignificant beeps."

"I don't think so."

"I'll prove it to you. After I wipe its primary memory botspeak will be no more."

"NO, you can't kill it!"

"Kill it? It's not alive! It's a nanobot! For goodness sake, there's nothing to kill."

Berto reached into the bot and twisted two pins. The bot started squeaking and beeping. Dee was beside himself.

"Listen to that!" Dee shouted.

"It's malfunctioning, that's all."

"No it's not. You're hurting it! STOP IT, BERTO!"

Berto continued. In a few moments, the primary would be out and the bot's memory would be history. He was just about to lift the core from its casing when Dee screamed, "NOOOOOOOO!"

Tension

Dee grabbed Berto's arm. Berto, slammed his free hand on the table and then used it to push Dee back. That did it; the stress of too much work, not enough sleep and endless worries about bots had finally gotten to them. They started to fight. Berto tried to get to the bot. Dee held him back. They wrestled to the ground. Berto pinned down Dee. Someone was getting ready to bust somebody in the teeth when Gunderson ran out of his office.

"Okay, ENOUGH!" He called to them, but they weren't listening. They just kept going at.

I ran over and helped Dr. Gunderson pull Berto off of Dee. It was not pretty. Dee had a bloody nose. One of Berto's ears was red.

"What's gotten into you guys?" Gunderson was mad at first but soon turned fatherly. He put his hand on both their heads and pulled them together. "You two really need to cool off. I suggest you go shoot some hoops at the community center. Go on, get out of here. And don't come back till you're friends again."

Berto looked at Dee. "Sorry about the nose, Dee."

"Yeah, and I was just about finished remodeling your head."

They were walking toward the lab door when Gunderson called to them. "I changed my mind. I want you back here in three hours, friends or not."

After they left, Gunderson went over to the dissection table. He looked at the bot and shook his head. He reconnected the pins and went back to his office. He started scribbling.

Two hours later Dee and Berto were back at the lab. They weren't talking, but they weren't fighting either.

Gunderson came out of his office a few moments later. "Let's get back to work everyone. I want to review what we know so far."

Gunderson charted our progress on a whiteboard like cops trying to solve a case. Medibot

116

experiment 207 was successful in attacking and killing E-coli. Gunderson said that he was in the process of expanding the research to other bacteria when one or more medibot 207s escaped into Fred causing him to become patient zero. People all over the world were infected shortly thereafter. At some point, nanobots all over the world started behaving like medibots.

"Does that sound about right?" he asked. We nodded our heads. "Looks like we've got the who, what, where and when. The only thing we don't know is why and how?"

Things were getting tense again. I could see worry in Gunderson's eyes. He was looking a little fried around the edges, like if we didn't figure out something soon he might lose it. I kind of wished he would lose it. Gunderson had lots of self-control and no observable temper. He kept things nicely bottled up inside. That worried me. Better to let off a little steam now and again. It seemed to work for Berto and Dee. Gunderson could be a balloon ready to pop. I had read about such things happening to people in our line of work. It's understandable, really. You think you know how life is put together and then, all of a sudden, you don't know anything. You've never prepared yourself for that possibility and... you lose it.

We all waited for Gunderson to either lose it or give us our next orders. Instead, he just walked into his office. Gunderson rested his elbows on his desk and placed his head in his hands. Maybe he was losing it quietly. If so, we thought it best not to bother him.

While we waited for Gunderson to reappear, I went through my training modules. I started with goal review. I had been doing resistance training in the tram on the way to MECHS in the morning. There was rarely anyone else there at that hour of the day so I had the whole car to myself. I used the overhead poles on the tram for pull-ups. I even found low ones for dips. There were vertical bars near the tram doors I could use to push away from or pull myself towards depending on how I angled my body. I made a fairly good score being creative.

I went ahead and set new goals for the week. I remembered that my dad had some bungee cords in our utility room. I thought I could tie a couple of them together and use them to build strength in my body. Lots of fancy exercise machines used elastic bands for the same thing. I started realizing that you don't need money to stay in shape.

Hours passed. Gunderson sat at his desk. No one wanted to bother him. He looked like he was making some notes on a pad, or maybe some kind of drawing. I couldn't tell what it was. We played LEDGE for a while but I couldn't concentrate. I wanted to know what Gunderson was thinking. We all wanted to know. Even Dee looked worried, and he was the one person around here who probably did know what was going through Gunderson's mind. I decided to test Dee's powers a bit.

"Dee," I asked. "Can you tell what's going on inside Dr. Gunderson's head right now? What's he up to?"

Dee had a worried look on his face, like he knew something but wouldn't say. He shook his head without answering.

I looked at my Vitalink to see what behavior change model was up next. It was something called PA WITH NO TRANSPORTATION. Apparently a lot of trainees offered not having wheels as an excuse for skipping exercise. They would say they couldn't get to the gym or the park or the whatever. As I've come to learn at MECHS, there are no good excuses, just barriers that all of us are capable of overcoming. The truth is that you can exercise anywhere, anytime. You just have to want to.

The PA module showed a number of situations in which a common form of transportation had been interrupted or was not available for one reason or another. Like the tram breaks down in the neighborhood, or your parents can't drive you to the gym because their car is broken down, or maybe they don't have a car. So the trainee is presented with the problem: how to get where you need to go to exercise? If you don't come up with the answer within a reasonable amount of time, the Vitalink pops up a menu with a number of possibilities. You would think that the first thing to come to a person's mind in a situation like this was walking. You'd be wrong. Most people didn't think about walking. There were other possibilities too. You could ask a neighbor to give you a ride. You could skateboard or maybe ride your bike. Stuff like that. Anyway I was just trying to keep myself busy until I knew what I was supposed to do.

"What do you think he's doing in there, Dee?" Elena also figured Dee could read Gunderson's mind from behind the closed door.

"I really don't know," Dee responded.

"You don't know?" Berto acted surprised. "What's the matter? Cat got your intuition?"

"Knock it off, Berto." Jessie snapped.

"Look Jessie," Berto said, "all I know is that it's a waste of time to go in for another bot. We should be doing hard science instead of chasing the fantasies of a so-called psychic."

"I thought I asked you two to stop bickering." Gunderson came out of his office looking a little better. He had a wad of papers in his hand. "I've looked over everything. My notes from the 207 experiment don't show anything new. This should not have happened. The medibots did exactly what I expected them to do. They were getting rid of disease not causing it. I must have missed something. I swear for the life of me I don't know what." He paused for several moments. He looked at Fred and then at the rest of us. He hesitated for a moment before he spoke. "Let's get ready for another mission. Berto, I know you think it's a waste of time, but we are going in anyway. I expect your full support."

"Of course," Berto said.

He turned his attention to Jessie and me. "I want you two to check your EB before you reduce this time. If you're balanced, I want you to tip the scales. I want you to have more energy since you're burning so much during molecular anatomy reduction. Lord knows what these missions are doing to Fred. Add some good protein and clean carbs. Have Berto make you a smoothie. That's probably the best thing for you."

Berto made us one of his super green concoctions. "This actually tastes better than it looks," he reassured us, "and it's just what the doctor ordered."

He was right, it was great. We drank our smoothies, suited up and climbed into the Flyer. Gunderson fired up the MARS. The Flyer shrunk down just like before, but the ride through the tube this time was calm, smooth and peaceful.

"Hey, Elena," Jessie called over the radio, "the stabilizers are working a lot better."

"Glad to hear it, Jess."

The Flyer came to a stop when we entered Fred's throat. We weren't there but a few minutes when a mass of bots swarmed to greet us. Jessie started sweating a little, but she was much better than before.

"Try to grab one, Wings," she said. I'll keep the Flyer steady."

"Alright," I said, "but do you mind if I try this first? I brought an audio clip of botspeak. Dee thought if we played it for the bots they might respond somehow?"

"I don't like detouring from the plan but I guess it's in line with the mission." Jessie gave me the go ahead.

I played the clip over the external sound system. *Schwee—peep—be—ba—da—beep—beep—beep*. It was Dee's voice. He was speaking bot, I guess.

Peep—be—ba—da—beep—beep. The bots responded in kind.

"Do you hear that Dee?" I called over the radio

"Loud and clear. It's incredible. I wish I knew what they were saying." Dee was excited.

I thought I could use Dee' audio clip to distract the bots while I came up behind one of them with the claw but they were too smart. The minute I engaged the claw they bolted. Jessie hit the throttle and started the chase. The simulator hadn't prepared me for this.

We were going incredibly fast. Climbing one minute and diving the next. We were flying through small slits with wavy, curtain-like phalanges, and then wave riding across sand dune-like landscapes. I was getting dizzy.

I kept grabbing at bots with no luck. They were way too fast. All of a sudden the swarm took a hard right and disappeared into a small hole. The Flyer was too big to fit through. Jessie brought the ship to a stop just outside the capillary.

"Now what?" I asked.

Neither one of us said a word for a long time. Then Jessie spoke. "I'm going EVA. You stay here and monitor me on the shipcam. I'll go in on foot. The camera in my helmet should pick up everything fairly well. Hand me the portable claw behind your seat, please."

"But what about your... you know. Maybe I should do it." I said.

"Yes I do know, but I gotta try." Jessie's voice was calm and cool. "I'm the one with the most Extra Vehicular Activity experience. I'm going in."

We put on our helmets. Jessie depressurized the Flyer, which allowed the outside plasma to fill the cockpit. I opened the canopy as Jessie climbed out. She had the claw in one hand and her Vitalink in the other. I buttoned up and repressurized the Flyer as I watched her move out of sight.

"Jessie? Do you read me? Come in." It was Gunderson.

"Yes, sir. We read you," I answered. "Jessie is tracking bots on foot. I repeat. Jessie is tracking bots on foot."

"What?" Gunderson was pretty excited. "Tell her to get back into the Flyer now! No EVAs. Do you hear me? Absolutely NO EVAs!"

"Yes, sir." I called Jessie on her radio. "Jessie, Gunderson says don't go in. Come back to the Flyer and let's get out of here."

No response. "Hey, do you hear me, Jessie?"

"Yeah, I hear you loud and clear," she said. "But I'm not coming back without a bot."

"It's an order, Jessie. Gunderson sounds mad."

"Fred's life is at stake. I am going to get us another bot!"

Gunderson kept calling. I kept asking Jessie to come back to the ship, but she wasn't listening.

Jessie radioed her progress. "I'm approaching the capillary the bots went into. I can't see too well. It's a little murky around here. I'm climbing in now. I've got one foot through. I can feel some sort of floor with my foot. I don't know... it's soft, not too stable."

I noticed something on the scanner. Back at MECHS, Berto had noticed it too.

"Somebody, come in," Berto called. "Wings, do you see something on your scanner?"

I called to Jessie. "Jessie, do you hear me? There's something ahead of you about ten meters at your scale.

"I can't see a thing, but I'm starting to hear something through my helmet. Sounds like bots." she said.

Jessie was right. I heard a series of sharp high pitch tones coming from inside the hole Jessie had just walked through. More botspeak but, this time, it sounded angry. The closer Jessie got to them, the angrier the sound.

"Get out Jessie, now!" I said. "I don't like the sound of this."

"Jessie, it's Dee. You don't have to do this. We'll find another way." Dee was pleading with her.

Gunderson called out as well, "For goodness sake abort the mission, Jessie. Please."

"It's all my fault, Dr. Gunderson. I'm not leaving without a bot."

Nanobots were closing in. The Flyer's sensors reported the claw was positioned near a bot. Jessie's helmet camera showed the claw open and swinging toward a bot. All of a sudden, the camera went dark and Jessie disappeared from the sensors. I made another scanner sweep. There was no sign of her. No sign of the bots either. Everything was dead quiet. The only thing I could hear was Gunderson crying out through my headset, "Jessieeeeee!"

Casualty

I went into automatic mode. I depressurized the Flyer, jumped out and ran to the hole that swallowed Jessie. Just stick your head through first, I thought. Keep cool. See what's in there. There were no nanobots. There was nothing in sight. I walked in and found a steep drop, about 30 meters at my scale, straight down. I knelt and peered over the top. I switched both of my helmet searchlights to full. At the bottom of the pit was Jessie's respirator, but there was no sign of Jessie. I scanned the pit with my Vitalink. No readings of any kind. Where was she?

I ran back to the Flyer and called the lab. "Do you have Jessie on your scanner?" They did not. I ran back to the hole and looked again. I scanned again. Still no sign of Jessie or nanobots. I felt my heart sink into my stomach.

I jumped into the Flyer and raced back to the lab. When I got there, everyone was freaking out. Gunderson was sick with worry. No one was saying it, but I was sure we were all thinking the same thing: how could Jessie survive without her respirator pack? We all knew she couldn't.

Gunderson immediately sent Berto and me back to look for Jessie. Berto had lots of EVA training, almost as much as Jessie. The two of us could accomplish more than me alone.

I put the Flyer into slow drive to minimize attracting bots. The trip back seemed to take forever. For some reason, I don't know why, Berto suggested I review my goals for the week.

"Oh for crying out loud, you have got to be kidding." I said. "Berto, I don't think this is the time for..."

"This will focus our minds on our mission," he said. "Trust me." The ever cool, ever calculating Berto was working the numbers.

I know, you probably think it's strange to be doing basic training activities while on a recovery mission, but Berto was right. It calmed me way down, allowing me to think more clearly about what I was doing.

The Flyer followed its program back to the location where Jessie disappeared. Berto reset my respirator. He explained that with the adjustment, it would give me some added mobility. We could use some of our oxygen as propellant. This would make the respirator capable of functioning like a jetpack, which could help us fly out of tight spots. That's good, I thought. I had a feeling we were walking into a tight spot.

As soon as we exited the ship we got an erratic signal from Jessie's transponder. We climbed through the opening where she disappeared and followed the signal. It was sort of like skydiving through gelatin. On the way down we looked everywhere. No luck, no sign of Jessie.

Once we hit bottom the signal got louder. Berto reached down and pulled up the mangled bits of metal that was Jessie's respirator. It was beaten up badly and the transponder inside it was smashed.

"Berto!" It was Dee on the radio. "I read a huge swarm of nanobots headed your way. They're half a click, your scale, and closing fast!"

"Roger that, Dee. I'm setting the backpacks to jump. Wings, follow me."

I saw the bots as soon we reached the top of the pit. We literally flew back to the ship with nanobots hot on our heels.

Berto jumped in the Flyer head first, hitting his helmet on the communications console. I did an emergency close on the cockpit canopy and punched us out of there. We zoomed out in high gear.

The landscape of the human body was like nothing you'd ever see anywhere else. For one thing, you can never be sure exactly where you are. Landmarks all look alike. Fortunately, we could track the ship's position on its scanner. There was a diagram of Fred's body with a flashing red dot that represented our flight pattern. Behind us was a smudge representing the swarm of nanobots following us. They had matched our speed and course, but they were not closing. Wonder why? I thought. They could probably outrun us if they wanted to. Maybe they can't? Or, maybe they don't want to?

Turbulence in the blood stream changed depending on where you were. Blood vessels and veins were like fast moving rivers. Once you entered the heart it was like being in a washing machine. The nervous system was like a static lightning storm—a spectacular fireworks show that could rival anything you could see on the fourth of July.

We were flying through Fred's body with the swarm of bots right behind us. I had the urge to stop, turn the Flyer around and go after one of them. Better not, I thought to myself. There's been enough trouble today. Best to lose them. I looked at the monitor and saw that I was in a main artery. The artery branched off into several smaller ones. I zeroed in on the one with the sharpest turn and programmed the Flyer for a maneuver I hoped would throw them off our trail. I never tried to outrun a bot before. I put the ship into Run mode and held on tight. I watched the monitor.

"What are you doing?" Berto cried out. "You're going to crash us."

"No I'm not. Just hold on."

I held the Flyer steady. I could see the turn right ahead of me. Okay, so maybe I was a little crazy, what with all the adrenaline pumping through me at the time, but it was the only thing I could think of. The countdown meter was approaching the final ten seconds... nine... eight... I clinched my teeth... five... four... three... I could feel the Flyer shifting gears... two... one.

Everything happened fast. When I opened my eyes and looked behind us the bots were gone. "Now let's get out of here before they come back." I called to Dee. "Bring us home, please." The MARS started its quantum magnification reentry program.

I felt sick to my stomach during the reentry. I kept going in and out of consciousness. Right before we materialized in the lab everything went blank. I must have passed out or something, even though I could hear people talking all around me.

"Get Wings to the Vitascan," someone said.

"Check the EB!"

"What happened?

"I don't know."

"Pulse is low..."

I felt myself floating, like a helium balloon released in the sky.

"We are losing Wings! Okay, shock advised. I am going to shock now! Stand clear everyone..."

There was a loud sound from somewhere.

"Charging. Stand clear!"

I felt my chest rise from the table and then slam back down. I kept trying to float upward but an invisible force was pulling me back. I struggled with it for a while and then I let go. When I hit the table my eyes snapped open. My head hurt badly. I looked up and found everyone hunched over me. I managed to slur a question, "What's going on?"

"Oh, nothing. You were dead and now you're not." Dee said calmly.

"I should not have sent you on back-to-back missions with no down time," Gunderson said.

"You must have burned up a week's supply of energy."

The next thing I knew I was laying on the cot in the LifePad listening to environmental sound clips. Elena was sitting at my side. My eyes were so heavy. Before I fell back to sleep I managed to mumble, "Jessie?"

Elena took my hand. "Don't worry about a thing," she said. "Just rest." Then my nightmare came back.

A band of bots was dragging each member of the team over to an erupting volcano. The bots were angry. They threw us into hot molten lava. As we fell to our death I saw Gunderson screaming. He was next. Behind him was Jessie. She was alive. I heard her screaming, "Why did you leave me?" I tried to scream back but my mouth wouldn't open. I wanted to tell her that I didn't leave her—that I tried to find her. I didn't want her to die thinking that I had abandoned her. The bots pushed Gunderson and Jessie to the edge of the volcano. They tossed them in like a piece of meat being tossed to a pack of wild dogs. In minutes they were gone. We were all gone.

I was soaking wet when I awoke. It was three o'clock in the morning. Elena was still there, sitting in the LifePad's beanbag chair. "You okay?" she asked.

"I don't know," I replied. "Where am I?"

"You're in MECHS lab. You're undergoing decompression just like before."

"Oh. What are you doing here?"

"Gunderson asked me to stay and watch you."

"Oh."

"You want something to eat?"

"No."

"Can I get you anything?"

"No."

She kept her questions short and sweet. She knew I was having a hard time. She had her Vitalink out and a bunch of papers spread on the mattress, like she was working on some project or something.

"What are you doing?" I asked.

"Just trying to keep busy. I'm working with my day planner program."

"What?"

"It's a program that helps me figure out how to structure my day so I make sure I get in some kind of workout."

"Oh."

"You want to try it?"

"Yeah, later," I said.

"I think you'd enjoy doing this now. Why don't I just ask you some questions? It'll keep your mind off of other things for a while."

"I thought Dee was the empath." My head was starting to clear.

"Yeah, well I don't have to be psychic to know what's good for someone... Did you say you wanted to try this?"

"Okay." Jessie could be bullheaded but Elena could be relentless in her own way. I climbed out of the cot and walked over to the sink to wash my face. I stretched. Then I sat down next to Elena and picked up her Vitalink.

"It's a simple idea, but you would be surprised how time can get away from you. This program helps you do a little reality testing. We'll input everything that you know you have to get done during the week. Then we'll look at how much time it takes to do it."

I went through a typical week with Elena. The current crisis was still my number one priority. In addition, I had to keep up with my food and exercise goals. I had family obligations as well, like babysitting my little brother. On top of that I still had to study the T2 curriculum. And, yet another progress review couldn't be far away. So many things to do. So little time.

Elena input my data. For me to be successful in all areas, a single day would have to last twenty-eight hours. Naturally, that was impossible. It looked like there was no way to do it. I got a little aggravated.

"What do they expect us to do? We can't grow another four hours a day in a Petri dish."

"No, but you can learn how to combine activities and plan your days so you can meet your goals. The program will give you some suggestions. I'll print them out for you. You can look at them when you're feeling better."

"She's dead isn't she?" I couldn't hold it in any longer.

"No, she's not dead. I know Jessie. She's very smart and she never gives up." Elena was speaking in a very low voice.

"She can't survive without her respirator, Elena."

"I don't care. Jessie's resourceful.

"I hope you're right."

We sat in silence for the longest time. We both knew I was right. We were kidding ourselves if we thought she was alive. Still, we played along. Back in the lab, everything was just as quiet, sort of like the calm before the storm.

"You want some green tea?" Elena asked.

"Yeah, okay." I figured why not. Elena wouldn't take no for an answer anyway, and it gave us something to do.

I looked over the printout and then asked her to download the program into my Vitalink. The printout suggested I could exercise while babysitting. I got this image of me using my brother for a barbell. I laughed a little and then turned off my Vitalink.

I stared at the bottom of my teacup and contemplated the situation. It seemed ridiculous to try and keep up with everything. What difference did it make now? Why bother staying healthy and setting goals if the whole world would soon been destroyed?

I climbed back into the cot and fell asleep.

When I awoke the next morning Gunderson informed me that I would have to spend three or four days in the LifePad building back my strength. Apparently the double trip had taken a lot out of my EB. He told me he was worried also about Fred. The missions in and out of his body were wearing him down too.

I worked out a little every day with some of the resistance machines. I got tired easily so I had to take it slow. I did my goal review. It was okay but not great. I set a new goal with Elena's program, although I'm not sure why. I guess because we are trained never to stray from our program unless instructed otherwise, so I went ahead and set the goal. I liked the idea of using my brother for a barbell, so that's what I told the Vitalink I would do. Actually, I found lifting heavy books was better. But that's the way it went. I tried to do what I would normally do until I recuperated.

I spent four days in the LifePad. By then, most everyone had accepted that Jessie was probably gone. Most everyone except Elena, that is. People deal with tragedy in different ways. Some can't accept the truth so they don't. I think it's called denial.

"No more Flyer trips into Fred," Dr. Gunderson announced to the team. "We'll figure this out some other way." He was moving slower. I know he would never admit it, but he looked like he was about to give up, like he had finally had it. He went back into his office and continued working on whatever it was he was working on in there. At one point Berto asked Gunderson if he needed any help. Gunderson just looked at him and kept working. Berto took out his

Vitalink and went back to playing LEDGE. One by one, we followed suit. There was little excitement in our play. I died during the first few minutes of each game. I didn't care if I won or lost.

Dee also looked troubled, but in a different way. "I've got a bad feeling, ya'll." Just as the last syllable left his lips, Fred's alarm started blaring again, big time.

Gunderson bolted out of his office. "Elena, NOW!" Elena jumped on the Vitascan as Gunderson downloaded her energy profile. The alarm continued.

"No way! I've been meeting all my goals!" Elena protested.

Berto jumped on next. The alarm continued. I tried and so did Dee. Fred's alarm kept ringing. The energy meter above the hydrotank flashed CRITICAL. The energy transfers were no longer working. We had just lost Jessie. Now we were about to lose Fred.

The Bomb

The President called on the videophone. "It's been a while since we've spoken, Dr. Gunderson. The folks around here are getting more and more anxious by the minute. What's happening at MECHS? I need a status report."

"We're losing him. He's been in there too long."

"What? Losing who?"

"Fred."

"Your pilot? The boy in the tank? I'm so sorry, Earl. I hate to ask you at a time like this but I have to know if there are any new developments?"

"New developments? Well yes, we've lost Jessie, my team leader, and Fred's gone critical. Madame President, we're a little busy right now. Thank you for calling." Gunderson was about to hang up on the president.

"Earl," the president interrupted, "what can we do to help? Just name it. The Joint Chiefs have offered..."

"I need only to be left alone right now, Margaret." Gunderson pointed to Fred in the hydrotank. "There's only one thing left to try. If this works we may have a breakthrough. If it doesn't..."

Gunderson and the president stared at each other for a long time. You could see concern in both faces. The president shook her head and then said, "Okay Earl, do what you can. Do everything you can."

"I will Madame President." Gunderson looked at her until she faded from the monitor. He turned to us and said, "Get the Flyer ready."

"I thought you said... Yes, sir." Berto snapped to attention. "Should I take Dee with me this time, sir?"

"No." Gunderson responded. "You aren't going anywhere. I am."

None of us knew what he was up to. He went back to his office. We knew he was working on something but no one knew what. By the looks of things it was important.

Fred's alarm continued to sound in the background. Dee went over to the bot table and started to reassemble the bot.

"What do you think you're doing?" Berto questioned.

"Just leave me alone. Okay?" Dee said.

"Sure, have at it. It doesn't make any difference anyway."

Gunderson reentered the lab. He was in his flight suit and carrying something heavy in his arms.

"What's that sir?" Elena asked.

"It's a free radical oxygen dispenser."

"You mean it's a reactive bomb?" Dee said.

"You're going to set off a bomb in Fred?" Elena was stunned.

"Not exactly. I will take the Flyer into Fred and place this dispenser near the swarm's last reported position. But it's not going to explode. It dispenses free radical oxygen. It's designed to destroy nanotechnology, not human tissue. It shouldn't hurt Fred."

"But what about Jessie?" Elena protested. "Her suit is nanotechnology!"

Gunderson put the dispenser down and walked over to Elena. He put his hands on her shoulders. "She's gone, Elena. There is no way Jessie could have survived."

"You don't know that for sure." Elena was crying.

"I'm afraid I do." Gunderson held up the dispenser. "This is the only thing we've got left. We are out of options and time. If I don't try it right now, we will lose Fred. Even if it works we could still lose him, but we might be able to save others. This may be the cure."

Gunderson climbed into the Flyer. Berto and I manned the flight console. "It's got a five-minute fuse, just enough time for me to set the timer and get out." Berto switched on the MARS. The Flyer and Gunderson disappeared.

Dee's bot came to life moments later and started squeaking to high heaven. It was struggling to release itself from the table's restraining field.

*Schwee–peep–be–ba–da–beep–beep–beep.
Schwee–peep–be–ba–da–beep–beep–beep!*

"Shut that thing up, will ya Dee!" Berto shouted.

"It is trying to say something. I just know it." "It's called random noise," Berto repeated.

146

"No, its not. It's a pattern. Listen!"

Schwee–peep–be–ba–da–beep–beep–beep. Schwee–peep–be–ba–da–beep–beep–beep. Schwee–peep–be–ba–da–beep–beep–beep.

To this day I don't know why but, Berto listened closely to the bot. Berto's eyes opened wide as he used his fingers to count the tones. Dee was right. It was a pattern. And it was repeating. It was not random. Berto started making calculations on his Vitalink.

"What is it?" Dee asked.

"Shhhhh. It's binary code." He kept calculating. "Well I'll be a bot's uncle. You're right, Dee. The little sucker is saying something."

"But what is it saying, Berto?" I asked.

"I have no idea, Wings."

"MECHS, do you read me? Come in!" It was Gunderson on the radio.

Elena went over to the flight console. "We read you loud and clear, sir."

"Come in Elena! Do you read me?" Gunderson called out again.

"Yes, sir, we read you loud and clear. Come in!"

Gunderson kept calling. Elena kept responding. It was obvious that he could not hear us. The Flyer's communication system had been damaged.

"I didn't get to check out the Flyer before he split." Elena said. "The shipcom must have gotten damaged somehow. The onboard camera link is out too."

Schwee–peep–be–ba–da–beep–beep–beep. The bot kept beeping.

I walked over to the Vitascan. "Look at this. Look at the swarm in Fred. What's going on?"

There was definitely something going on. We could see the Flyer and Gunderson on the Vitascan. The swarm also had noticed his presence.

"What's Gunderson doing?" I asked.

"He's planting the bomb," Berto responded.

The bot in the lab was freaking out. The swarm on the Vitascan monitor was flashing like a Christmas tree. It looked they were heading right toward Gunderson.

"I'm exiting the ship... I have the dispenser..."

Gunderson was talking us through his maneuver. He knew we couldn't hear him. He was doing it for the record. It was standard procedure.

148

"Try the Flyer's cam!" Berto shouted.

"It's not working yet! I'm trying to fix it," Elena shot back.

The bot on the table finally broke loose and took off. It was soon circling Fred high above the hydrotank.

"It's attacking Fred!" I yelled.

"No it's not," Berto said. "Leave it alone, Wings. Hey Dee, let's try this. See if you can persuade your bot to come down from the ceiling. We'll try talking to it."

Dee did as Berto asked. Then Berto asked the bot a series of questions. "Listen 207, no equals zero beeps, yes equals one beep. Do you understand me?"

The bot emitted a single beep. We all looked at each other, astonished.

"Are you a nanobot?" Berto asked

"Beep."

"Are you a dog?" The bot was silent.

"I owe you a big apology, Dee." Berto said.

"Why did you make Fred sick?" Elena asked. The bot did not respond.

"Yes or no questions only," Berto reminded everyone. The inquisition continued until it was clear that nanobots had nothing to do with Fred getting sick. It took fifteen or twenty yes/no questions to start making sense out of all this.

"If I'm understanding things correctly," Berto summarized, "the bot is saying the reason it went into Fred is because it thought Fred was sick. Gunderson programmed these guys to find and cure disease, so that's what they did. The bots were just doing their job."

"What disease did they think Fred had?" I asked.

We were scratching our heads when Elena riffled through a stack of files. She was looking through a bunch of records when she pulled out Fred's Vitalink and plugged it into the Vitascan. She downloaded his data and walked over to the monitor. "That's it!"

"What's it?" I said.

"We didn't go back far enough with Fred's data. We should have looked at his biosensor before he passed out."

"Why?" Berto questioned.

"Look at the screen." Elena pointed to a simulated representation of Fred's insides. The data from his Vitalink reflected what was going on in Fred prior to his passing out. An area in his abdomen was highlighted in red. "Something was going on inside of him, right here in the pancreas, before the bots arrived. And whatever it was, it got really bad at *Eaties.* That's when the bots went to work on Fred!"

"So... they must have been riding him until they sensed he needed help," Dee deduced.

"Beep." The bot responded.

"I have placed the bomb near a vein wall," Gunderson said over the radio. "I am preparing to set the bomb."

"Dr. Gunderson!" Dee shouted. "We have got to stop him! He's going to kill the bots! It's not the bots!"

"Beep!" The bot's tone was getting louder.

Gunderson continued, "I have set the bomb and started the timer. In five minutes this nightmare will be over."

Countdown

We could see Gunderson's position on the Vitascan. We could also see what he couldn't— thousands of bots were assembling in back of him. He was about to be attacked by the whole nanoswarm. There was nothing we could do. Berto kept trying to call him without luck.

Elena pointed to something else in Fred's Vitascan data. "Look. It's a glucose marker. He had an unhealthy concentration of glucose in his system when he passed out.

"We were so busy looking at the bots that we missed the obvious," Dee chimed in.

It wasn't the bots after all. The 207s were doing what they were programmed to do. But it still didn't explain why the other bots were ignoring their original programming.

"I got it! The camera is working!" Elena screamed. I was glad to see Gunderson's image on the monitor.

"Look!" Berto said. The bots were moving in on Gunderson. He tried to make it back to the Flyer but was blocked by a wall of bots. He was surrounded.

"Get OUT of my way!" Gunderson was yelling into his microphone. "Why? WHY DID YOU TURN ON ME?" Gunderson's anger was off the chart. Now, he was losing it.

We kept trying to reach him. In his attempt to cure all disease, Gunderson was about to destroy the only thing ever designed for that single purpose. What Gunderson didn't know was his creation was working perfectly. But the bomb was still ticking down. There was no way he could get out now in time to save himself. Gunderson would go down with his bots. Fred's condition was still critical and getting worse. It was like one of those bad movies where everyone dies in the end - the end of the world as far as I could tell.

I had to do something. Anything. I ran into Dr. Gunderson's office and started looking through the papers around his desk. Dee's bot followed me in. How could Gunderson work in here? There were towers of papers, reams and reams stacked five or six feet high all over the place. It was like a forest of paper stack trees. There was barely enough room to stand, much less—and then I found it. A small folder under a large pile labeled FREE RADICAL OXYGEN DISPENSER. I grabbed the folder and a small drawing dropped out. A schematic diagram of the bomb? The bot and I were looking it over when we heard Berto say something back in the lab. I ran out of the office. "Now what's happening?"

Berto directed our attention to something else on the Vitascan monitor, something not registering as a nanobot. It wasn't visible on the Flyer's camera because it was deep in the middle of the swarm. Slowly, it was moving toward the ship.

The bots were literally on top of Gunderson. The bomb was approaching its final minute. Suddenly, our monitor showed the swarm parting like a curtain. Two bots moved forward. They were carrying something much larger than them. As they got closer to the camera you could see it was someone in a flight suit and helmet.

"Dr. Gunderson!" It was Jessie's voice.

"Jessie? I can't believe it!" Gunderson cried out.

We couldn't believe it either. Jessie was alive.

"I broke my leg and probably a few ribs when I fell," she said. "The bots set my leg and they've been working very hard to make sure I stay healthy."

"But your respirator? How...?"

"It smashed when I fell. I thought I was a goner, but they've been harvesting oxygen from Fred's lungs and injecting it into my suit."

Gunderson suddenly remembered the dispenser. He turned to look down at the device near his foot. "The bomb! What have I done? We'll never make it out of here in time!"

Gunderson tried to shut down the timer but it ignored him. At T-minus one minute, the bomb's fuse was programmed to go into auto mode. The off switch was locked out. Gunderson removed an access panel and tried to pull out a wire. Unfortunately, his glove was too large to fit into the access hole. T-minus 12 seconds... T-minus 11 seconds... T-minus...

Gunderson moved toward Jessie to protect her from the blast. A single nanobot moved alongside the bomb. There was a flash of light. Gunderson and

Jessie covered their heads to brace themselves. We did the same thing in the lab, holding on tight to one another as the timer's display turned from two seconds, to one second, to zero.

Berto let out a loud scream. "Ahhhhhhhh!"

We held tight for several seconds. Nothing happened. We waited. Still nothing. We looked again at the monitor.

The single bot near the bomb lifted something up and maneuvered to where Gunderson and Jessie were crouching. Then it dropped the bomb's timer at Gunderson's feet. One of the wires had been surgically cut with great precision. The bot had diffused the bomb.

Gunderson and Jessie made their way to the Flyer and climbed in. Once we saw the canopy close, Elena and I ran over to the MARS to bring them home. Within five minutes the ship was back in the lab. Gunderson and Jessie stumbled out of the Flyer. We all ran over to help.

"We tried to reach you, but the shipcom was down!" Berto said.

"I know." Gunderson was helping Jessie stand. "Get her to the LifePad."

"Oh, Jessie, thank God you're alive." Elena embraced her friend. We all crowded around Jessie.

Berto took her vital signs. "You look pretty good, considering."

"What happened in there?" I asked.

"I damaged my respirator when I fell. The next thing I knew the bots were all around me. I tried to get up, but I couldn't. I knew I had broken my leg. I thought it was all over. I kept waiting for them to attack, but they never did. Instead they helped me. I was hoping you guys would come back and get me."

"We tried," Berto said. "We found your respirator. We knew you couldn't survive without it."

"Yeah, I can understand that."

"But how did you survive?" I asked.

"The bots supplied me with oxygen. I know this sounds weird, but they worked out a way for me to tap into Fred's lungs."

"It doesn't surprise me. These are intelligent bots; smarter than the Smart Germs they were designed to kill." Dr. Gunderson sounded like a proud parent.

Fred's alarm was still ringing in the background. Jessie turned to hydrotank. "What's happening to Fred?" Jessie tried to get up.

"We've got to get the bots out of him now," Gunderson said. "I've got another dispenser in my..."

"No, wait," Dee interrupted. "Jessie. Stay put. Dr. Gunderson, it wasn't the bots that made Fred sick. While you were gone we re-reviewed Fred's data. Look."

Dee pointed to Fred's scans. Gunderson took a close look. "Glucose. Of course! Now I get it. The bots spotted a problem in Fred. They couldn't distinguish the glucose buildup from a virus so they tried to fix it. That makes sense. But they really don't have the tools to fight glucose because having too much glucose is not a virus."

Gunderson smiled and put his arms around Berto and Dee. "You two figured this out?"

"Actually, it was Elena." Berto said.

"What about the other bots?" Gunderson was still puzzled. "You know, the ones that are not 207s?"

This time, Berto had the answer. "Dee was right. They were communicating with each other all along. When Jessie let the 207s out of the flask they went straight to work just like you programmed them to. Some of them landed in Fred. Some of them got into the wild on the way to *Eaties*. From there, they found other people with similar symptoms as Fred. Since there were only a few thousand 207s, they needed help. So, they called in their friends."

"I never figured on 207s finding a way to modify the hardcode of other bots," Gunderson said. "But that must be what they did. They transmitted their own code to other bots to help them to combat what they thought was a new Smart Germ."

"Wow," I said, "the bots invaded our bodies to try and save us from what they thought were Smart Germs, but they couldn't save us from ourselves. There was no virus to attack. We were doing this to ourselves. We were making ourselves sick by eating poorly and not exercising."

Gunderson called the President and told her the news. Things happened very quickly after that. The White House called the Global Council who then called national health agencies all over the world. Soon, every hospital was looking for glucose markers in nanobot patients. Fred's system had too much glucose, and it turned out most of the other patients had the same problem.

The solution was eating more healthy foods and increasing physical activity. In short, better diet and more exercise.

Unfortunately, Fred's problem was more severe than the other nanobot patients. His poor eating habits and lack of physical activity made the stress of the hydrotank and Flyer missions too much. He was also patient zero. The bots had been inside him longer than anyone else, and he had endured multiple Flyer missions inside him. He was way sicker than anyone else.

"You know, all this talk about glucose, diet and exercise is very interesting, but Fred's health meter alarm is still beeping!" Jessie's voice was desperate. Just then, Fred's meter fell to zero, then the flashing CRITICAL sign went dark. The beep turned into a long monotonous tone.

Gunderson ran to the hydrotank console and began frantically pushing buttons.

"What can we do?" Elena asked. "Should I get on the Vitascan?"

Gunderson looked at the displays for a long time as all other eyes looked at Gunderson. Finally, he touched a button on the console to turn off the alarm.

The tone went silent. "No, Elena. That won't help anymore. I'm afraid that's it, everyone. I'm very sorry."

"You mean he's..." Dee hesitated.

"No way!" Jessie shouted. "We are not giving up! This is far from over. Listen up everyone, we haven't got much time..."

Game Over

Jessie told Berto to get on the exercycle in the LifePad. Elena ran a patch from Berto's Vitalink to Fred. Jessie was hoping Berto could help burn up the glucose in Fred's system to stabilize him. No luck. Then the other team members linked to Fred, first Dee and then Elena. Like before, it wasn't enough. Gunderson told us it was too soon after the last mission. Jessie and Dr. Gunderson were too weak to do Fred any good. It was now up to me. Berto, Dee and Elena's energy were in. Maybe, if I could tip the scales, Fred might just pull out of it. Maybe.

All my training—all of my goals—were about to be put to the test. Fred's life was now in my hands. Gunderson told me to sync my Vitalink to Fred and download my cumulative results. All the points I had accumulated from goal setting, goal review, EB training, and weekly modules would now determine if Fred lived or died. I couldn't believe it would come to this. If I had known Fred's life was going to depend on me, I might have done things very differently.

But it was too late for that now. I jumped on the Vitascan and downloaded everything to Fred. At first, nothing. Fred's life meter was stuck at the bottom. It seemed like an eternity for the miracle to happen. When it did, 30 seconds later, a cheer rang out in the lab. Fred's meter started moving up, first slowly, then a little faster. Would it be enough to save him? I had no earthly idea.

Everyone was fixated on Fred's meter. Each time the needle moved up a notch, you could feel the tension in the room release a little. It was the longest ten minutes of my life. Gradually, looking at Fred's face through the hydrotank through his helmet, you could see the color coming back. Then alarm came back on. Fred was now CRITICAL, which was a lot better than being deceased. The alarm silenced when Fred's condition reached GOOD. It seemed as if I had done it. It seemed as if Fred was going to survive.

Three days later, Fred was out of the hydrotank and sitting next to us in the LifePad. We walked him through the whole adventure. Jessie told him how I took over as Flyer pilot for him. Fred was impressed with the stories of my flying, and that made me feel pretty good. I told Fred how Jessie walked alone into a bot swarm to save him. It was the bravest thing I had ever seen. Fred did not seem surprised.

"Does this mean you're over your fear of spiders, Tomahawk?" Fred asked.

"Yeah, it does." Jessie answer was full of confidence.

Fred looked at me, a little disappointed. Nobody to tease anymore, I figured. Then he asked, "Well, is there anything else important that I missed?"

Jessie grabbed Fred's chin and turned his head around to face her. She looked directly into his eyes and said, "Yes. Me!"

Epilogue

Of course, most training sessions at MECHS don't usually start off with an international crisis. Things generally run more smoothly. Still, I can't help but think that the experience in my first year shaped me into the person I am today.

Jessie and the others went on to do great things. Today they head their own MECHS departments. Berto leads a group of talented computer programmers. Dee teaches new trainees in what has come to be known as "applied clairvoyance." His techniques have become a part of standard training at MECHS. Elena became internationally recognized for contributions to the field of nanomechanics. She was awarded the Academe Prize for scientific advancement in 2060.

Of course, Jessie's Flyer technology revolutionized travel, completely replacing trams. She continued making improvements to Flyers over the years. Jessie recently completed the Flyer 2100 Project. This newest version of the ship flies hypersonic, something most scientists thought was impossible.

Fred's brush with death turned his life around. He became the model MECHS team member. Fit, lean and trim, the diet and exercise regimens he developed for new trainees are today part of school curricula all over the world.

Oh, and one more thing. Believe it or not, Fred and Jessie got married. Guess I should have seen that one coming.

Me? I still work in Gunderson's old lab, except that my name is now on the door. Yep, that's right. I'm the new MECHS chief of staff. Gunderson pops in once in a while. He's frail but manages to travel, lecturing and signing books. I call him from time to time to get advice about this and that, mostly about how to handle new trainees.

His advise to me is always the same. "Just tell them to eat right and exercise. Teach them to set goals and meet them. Life can really be that simple."

Yeah, it's hard to argue with that.

Acknowledgements

It would take a long time to list all the contributors to this story; there are well over a hundred. It took that many people because this novella is based on the children's video game for health, *Nanoswarm: Invasion From Inner Space*. More than based on, actually, this book was written to help the game developers fully understand the backstory and characters appearing in the video game.

It turned out to be such a good story that it couldn't be left to gather electronic dust on some hard drive. It needed to be in print.

Video games are large undertakings involving a team of producers, directors, writers, 3-d animators, game artists, computer programmers, musicians, actors, and on and on. A full accounting of the making of the *Nanoswarm* video game and all those due grateful appreciation will be the subject of another book. Until then, special thanks are due almost 100 talented individuals who spent five years making the Nanoswarm: Invasion From Inner Space serious game. It was a huge production, in particular, the cinematic cut scences shot with live actors on a huge blue screen sound stage. None of it would have been possible without the skill and experience of Bob Cozens, Director and Associate Producer Janet Benton.

Another special thank you goes to Freeman Williams for his story contributions to the project. Freeman conceived the original story idea and wrote the video game cinematic scripts, some of which reappear here. Thank you (again) to Janet Benton and to Ben McMahan for helpful story suggestions during the evolution of this book, and to Melanie Lazarus, MPH for editing reviews.

The making of *Nanoswarm* and the *Nanoswarm* storyline itself are interesting. But there is another message here also worth telling. The United Nations World Health Organization terms it, "globesity," the worldwide obesity epidemic that has become the single most important health issue of our time. Why is that?

Today, two-thirds of Americans are either overweight or obese, including more than 13 million overweight children. The rest of the world isn't far behind us. Being overweight is associated with numerous life-threatening diseases. To name a few: high blood pressure, heart disease, breast, colon, prostate and pancreatic cancers, and type II diabetes. Obesity is the second leading cause of death in the United States. Only cancer kills more Americans each year, and this will soon be surpassed by obesity.

Sound a little frightening? It should. Here's more to ponder. Thanks to obesity, it is predicted that today's kids will be the first American generation in hundreds of years whose lifespan will be shorter than their parents. One-third of all children born after 2000 are predicted to develop type II diabetes, a severe and expensive disease with no cure.

Recognition is, therefore, also due to our scientific collaborators at Houston's Children's Nutrition Research Center. The CNRC is a unique cooperative venture between Baylor College of

Medicine and the US Department of Agriculture/Agricultural Research Service. The groundbreaking work of Archimage's CNRC collaborators (Tom Baranowski, PhD; Debbe Thompson, PhD; Karen Cullen, PhD; Janice Baranowski, MPH, RD; and their staff) on video games for diet and exercise behavior change is a new chapter in this unfolding health care saga.

Grateful acknowledgement is also due the National Institute of Diabetes and Digestive and Kidney Diseases. Thank you Barbara Linder, MD and Sandy Garfield, PhD for your support in exploring new ways to combat the obesity epidemic.

Richard Buday, FAIA, President, Archimage

Mary Ann Pendino is a writer and actor. She began her career in the early 80s at The Comedy Workshop in Houston. Following an eight-year Workshop residency, she developed three popular one-woman shows and two musicals for Houston's Stages Repertory Theatre and Main Street Theater. Mary Ann has also been a copywriter for radio and television, and composed several original jingles. She has performed at numerous theaters throughout the US, including Second City in Chicago.

Richard Buday, FAIA is president and founder of Archimage, a 27-year-old digital arts design studio. A professional architect by training, Richard and his firm have won 50 international awards for design including broadcast television commercials; retail, commercial and health-related video games and interactive media; illustration and graphic design for corporate identity, magazine covers and print advertisements.

www.ingramcontent.com/pod-product-compliance
Lightning Source LLC
Chambersburg PA
CBHW051917240626
47153CB00004B/1264

* 9 780578 034973 *